WINTER'S BONE

WINTER'S
BONE

A Novel

Daniel Woodrell

LITTLE, BROWN AND COMPANY

New York   Boston

Little, Brown and Company
Time Warner Book Group
1271 Avenue of the Americas, New York, NY 10020
Visit our Web site at www.twbookmark.com

First Edition: August 2006

The characters and events in this book are fictitious. Any similarity to real persons, living or dead, is coincidental and not intended by the author.

Library of Congress Cataloging-in-Publication Data

Woodrell, Daniel.
    Winter's bone : a novel / Daniel Woodrell — 1st ed.
        p. cm.
    ISBN-10: 0-316-05755-X / ISBN-13: 978-0-316-05755-4
    1. Teenage girls — Fiction.   2. Fugitives from justice — Fiction.
    3. Fathers and daughters — Fiction.   4. Problem families — Fiction.
    5. Ozark Mountains — Fiction.   6. Rural families — Fiction.
    7. Mountain life — Fiction.   I. Title.

PS3573.O6263W56   2006
813'.54 — dc22   2005017349

10 9 8 7 6 5 4 3 2

Q-FF

Book design by Jo Anne Metsch

Printed in the United States of America

To Ellen Levine, stalwart again,

and Katie

To cover the houses and the
stones with green — so the
sky would make sense — you
have to push down black
roots into the dark.

—CESARE PAVESE

WINTER'S BONE

REE DOLLY stood at break of day on her cold front steps and smelled coming flurries and saw meat. Meat hung from trees across the creek. The carcasses hung pale of flesh with a fatty gleam from low limbs of saplings in the side yards. Three halt haggard houses formed a kneeling rank on the far creekside and each had two or more skinned torsos dangling by rope from sagged limbs, venison left to the weather for two nights and three days so the early blossoming of decay might round the flavor, sweeten that meat to the bone.

Snow clouds had replaced the horizon, capped the valley darkly, and chafing wind blew so the hung meat twirled from jigging branches. Ree, brunette and sixteen, with milk skin and abrupt green eyes, stood bare-armed in a fluttering yellowed dress, face to the wind, her cheeks reddening as if smacked and smacked again. She stood tall in combat boots, scarce at the waist but plenty through the arms and shoulders, a body made for loping after needs. She smelled the frosty wet in the looming clouds, thought of her shadowed kitchen and lean cupboard, looked to the scant woodpile, shuddered. The coming weather meant wash hung outside would freeze into planks, so she'd have to stretch clothesline across the kitchen above the woodstove, and the puny stack of wood split for the potbelly would not last long enough to dry much except Mom's underthings and maybe a few T-shirts for the boys. Ree knew there was no gas for the chain saw, so she'd be swinging the ax out back while winter blew into the valley and fell around her.

Jessup, her father, had not set by a fat woodpile nor split what there was for the potbelly before he went down the steep yard to his blue Capri and bounced away on the rut road. He had not set food by nor money, but promised he'd be back soon as he could with a paper sack of cash and a trunkload of delights. Jessup was a broken-faced, furtive man given to uttering quick pleading promises that made it easier for him to walk out the door and be gone, or come back inside and be forgiven.

Walnuts were still falling when Ree saw him last. Walnuts were thumping to ground in the night like stalking footsteps of some large thing that never quite came into view, and Jessup had paced on this porch in a worried slouch, dented nose snuffling, lantern jaw smoked by beard, eyes uncertain and alarmed by each walnut thump. The darkness and those thumps out in the darkness seemed to keep him jumpy. He paced until a decision popped into his head, then started down the steps, going fast into the night before his mind could change. He said, "Start lookin' for me soon as you see my face. 'Til then, don't even wonder."

She heard the door behind her squeak and Harold, age eight, dark and slight, stood in pale long johns, holding the knob, fidgeting from foot to foot. He raised his chin, gestured toward the meat trees across the creek.

"Maybe tonight Blond Milton'll bring us by one to eat."

"That could be."

"Don't kin ought to?"

"That's what is always said."

"Could be we should ask."

She looked at Harold, with his easy smile, black hair riffling in the wind, then snatched his nearest ear and twisted until his jaw fell loose and he raised his hand to swat at hers. She twisted until he bore up under the pain and stopped swatting.

"*Never.* Never ask for what ought to be offered."

"I'm cold," he said. He rubbed his smarting ear. "Is grits all we got?"

"Butter 'em more. There's still a tat of butter."

He held the door and they both stepped inside.

"No, there ain't."

MOM SAT in her chair beside the potbelly and the boys sat at the table eating what Ree fed them. Mom's morning pills turned her into a cat, a breathing thing that sat near heat and occasionally made a sound. Mom's chair was an old padded rocker that seldom rocked, and at odd instants she'd hum ill-matched snips of music, notes unrelated by melody or pitch. But for most of any day she was quiet and still, wearing a small lingering smile prompted by something vaguely nice going on inside her head. She was a Bromont, born to this house, and she'd once been pretty. Even as she was now, medicated and lost to the present, with hair she forgot to wash or brush and deep wrinkles growing on her face, you could see she'd once been as comely as any girl that ever danced barefoot across this tangled country of Ozark hills and hollers. Long, dark, and lovely she had been, in those days before her mind broke and the parts scattered and she let them go.

Ree said, "Finish up eatin'. Bus'll be along soon."

The house had been built in 1914, the ceilings were high, and the single light overhead threw dour shadows behind everything. Warped shadow-shapes lay all across the floor and walls and bulged in the corners. The house was cool in the brighter spots and chill in the shadows. Windows set high into the walls, and outside the panes torn plastic sheeting from the winter before whipped and fluttered. The furniture came into the house when Mamaw and Grandad Bromont were alive, had been in use since Mom was a child, and the lumpy stuffing and worn fabric yet held the scent of Grandad's pipe tobacco and ten thousand dusty days.

Ree stood at the sink rinsing dishes, looking out the window onto the sharp slope of bare trees, looming rock ledges and a thin mud trail. Storm wind shoved limbs around and whistled past the window frame, hooted down the stovepipe. The sky came into the valley low, glum and blustery, about to bust open and snow.

Sonny said, "These socks smell."

"Would you just put 'em on? You'll miss the bus."

Harold said, "My socks smell, too."

"Would you just *please, please, please* put those fuckin' socks on! Would you do that? Huh?"

Sonny and Harold were eighteen months apart in age. They nearly always went about shoulder to shoulder, running side by side and turning this way or veering that way at the same sudden instant, without a word, moving about in a spooky, instinctive tandem, like scampering quotation marks. Sonny, the older boy, was ten, seed from a brute, strong, hostile, and direct. His hair was the color of a fallen oak leaf, his fists made hard young knots, and he'd become a scrapper at school. Harold trailed Sonny and tried to do as he did, but lacked the same sort of punishing spirit and muscle and often came home in need of fixing, bruised or sprained or humiliated.

Harold said, "They don't really stink that bad, Ree."

Sonny said, "Yeah, they do. But it don't matter. They'll be in our boots."

Ree's grand hope was that these boys would not be dead to wonder by age twelve, dulled to life, empty of kindness, boiling with mean. So many Dolly kids were that way, ruined before they had chin hair, groomed to live outside square law and abide by the remorseless blood-soaked commandments that governed lives led outside square law. There were two hundred Dollys, plus Lockrums, Boshells, Tankerslys, and Langans, who were basically Dollys by marriage, living within thirty miles of this valley. Some lived square lives, many did not, but even the square-living Dollys were Dollys at heart and might be helpful kin in a pinch. The rough Dollys were plenty peppery and hard-boiled toward one another, but were unleashed hell on enemies, scornful of town law and town ways, clinging to their own. Sometimes when Ree fed Sonny and Harold oatmeal suppers they would cry, sit there spooning down oatmeal but crying for meat, eating all there was while crying for all there could be, become wailing little cyclones of want and need, and she would fear for them.

"Get," she said. "Get your book satchels'n get. Get down the road'n catch that bus. And put your stocking hats on."

THE SNOW fell first in hard little bits, frosty white bits blown sideways to pelt Ree's face as she raised the ax, swung down, raised it again, splitting wood while being stung by cold flung from the sky. Bits worked inside her neckline and melted against her chest. Ree's hair was shoulder-length and full, with ungovernable loose curls from temples to neck and snow bits gathered in the tangle. Her overcoat was an implacable black and had been Mamaw's, grim old wool battered by decades of howling winter and summer moths. The buttonless coat fell past her knees, below her dress, but draped open and did not hamper her chopping strokes. Her swings were practiced and powerful, short potent whacks. Splinters flew, wood split, the pile grew. Ree's nose ran and the blood came up in her face and made pink on her cheeks. She pinched two fingers high on her nose, snorted a splat to the ground, dragged a sleeve across her face, swung the ax again.

Once the pile of splits became big enough to sit on, she did. She sat with her long legs close beneath her, booted feet spread wide, pulled headphones from a pocket and clamped them over her ears, then turned on *The Sounds of Tranquil*

Shores. While frosty bits gathered in her hair and on her shoulders she raised the volume of those ocean sounds. Ree needed often to inject herself with pleasant sounds, stab those sounds past the constant screeching, squalling hubbub regular life raised inside her spirit, poke the soothing sounds past that racket and down deep where her jittering soul paced on a stone slab in a gray room, agitated and endlessly provoked but yearning to hear something that might bring a moment's rest. The tapes had been given to Mom who already heard too many puzzling sounds and did not care to confront these, but Ree tried them and felt something unknot. She also favored *The Sounds of Tranquil Streams, The Sounds of Tropical Dawn,* and *Alpine Dusk.*

As the frosty bits dwindled the wind slowed and big snowflakes began falling as serenely as anything could fall the distance from the sky. Ree listened to lapping waves of far shores while snowflakes gathered on her. She sat unmoving and let snow etch her outline in deepening clean whiteness. The valley seemed in twilight though it was not yet noon. The three houses across the creek put on white shawls and burning lights squinted golden from the windows. Meat still hung from limbs in the side yards, and snow began clinging to the limbs and meat. Ocean waves kept sighing to shore while snow built everywhere she could see.

Headlights came into the valley on the rut road. Ree felt a sudden bounce of hope and stood. The car had to be coming here, the road ended here. She pulled the headphones to her neck and slid down the slope toward the road. Her boots left skid tracks in the snow and she fell on her ass near the bottom, then raised to her knees and saw that it was the law, a sheriff's car. Two little heads looked out from the backseat.

Ree knelt beneath stripped walnut trees, watching as the car cut long scars in the fresh snow, pulled near and stopped. She pushed to her feet and rushed around the hood to the driver's side, taking firm aggressive strides. When the door cracked open, she leaned and said, *"They didn't do nothin'! They didn't do a goddamned thing! What the hell're you tryin' to pull?"*

A rear door opened and the boys slid out laughing until they heard Ree's tone and saw her expression. The glee drained from their faces and they became still. The deputy stood, raised his hands, showed her his palms, shook his head.

"Hold your beans, girl — I just brung 'em down from where the bus stopped. This snow has shut the school. Just give 'em a ride is all."

She felt heat rise in her neck and cheeks, but turned to the boys, hands on her hips.

"You boys don't need to do no ridin' around with the law. Hear me? The walk ain't that far." She glanced across the creek, saw curtains parted, shapes moving. She pointed up the slope to the woodpile. "Now get up there and bring them splits into the kitchen. *Go.*"

The deputy said, "I was on my way here, anyhow."

"Now why in hell would that be?"

Ree knew the deputy's name was Baskin. He was short but wide, said to be a John Law nobody should tangle with unless the stakes were high, quick to draw, quicker to club. These country deputies answered calls alone, with backup help an hour or more away, so dainty rules and regulations were not first on their list of things to worry about. Or second, either. Baskin's wife was a Tankersly from Haslam Springs, and Mom had gone to school with her from first grade on up and had still been friendly with her until they both married. Baskin had arrested Jessup on the porch late in the summer past.

"Ask me inside," he said. He dusted snow from his shoulders. "I got to talk some with your momma."

"She ain't in the mood."

"Ask me in, or watch me go in, anyhow. Whichever way you like it best."

"Goin' to be like that, huh?"

"Listen, I didn't drive close on two hours of bad road only just to see your smilin' face, girl. I got reasons. Ask me in or follow, it's goddam cold out here."

He began moving toward the porch and Ree loped ahead of him and stopped him at the door.

"Stomp your shoes. Don't track melt all over my floor."

Baskin stalled and hung his head for a moment, like a bull pondering, then nodded and dramatically stomped the snow from his feet. He made porch planks wiggle, snow fall from the railings, sent booms into the valley. "Good enough?"

She shrugged but held the door for him, slammed it shut as his heels cleared the threshold. Clothes were strung in three ranks across the kitchen, shirts drooping to eye level, dresses and pants falling deeper from the lines. Drips formed puddles beneath the thicker garments and trickles followed the slant of the floor to the wall. It was easiest to move about through sections where underthings and socks allowed more headroom. Mom sat in her chair beside the potbelly, humming thoughtlessly until she saw Baskin ducking below her damp panties.

"Not in my daddy's house!" She smiled broadly, as if tickled by the surprise antics of a likable idiot. She began to rock her chair and laughed and held her eyes nearly closed. "Huh-uh, huh-uh. No, sir." She pouted her lips, shook her head, suddenly dulled again. "You can't bust a girl in her *own daddy's house.*" She did not look at Baskin, but bowed her head and raised her knees to her chest and folded herself into a posture of tormented penance meekly offered. "I seen it written. Over there, somewhere. Daddy's house ain't the one you can do nothin' in."

Ree watched Baskin's face spin through reactions: brief alarm, then confusion, sadness, resignation, pity. She waited until he turned from Mom, stumped and flubbing his lips. She said, "Just tell me."

The boys came in from the back, cheeks looking scuffed red by cold, hair damp, and dropped armloads of splits that clattered beside the potbelly. Some splits carried snow and thawed more wet onto the floor. The boys went for another load and Baskin nodded after them, saying, "Could be we should talk on the porch."

"That bad, huh?"

"Not yet. Not for sure. But you never do know."

The porch was surrounded by a shifting veil of falling snow. Ree and Baskin stood awkwardly and silent for a time, the breath from both rising white toward the passing flakes. Dollys across the creek gathered near the meat trees in their side yards, big knives in hand, slashing at ropes so the hanging meat would drop to ground. Several times Blond Milton and Sonya and the others paused in their slashing and looked toward the porch.

"You know Jessup's out on bond, don't you?"

"So what?"

"You know he cooks crank, don't you?"

"I know that's the charges you laid against him. But you ain't proved it on him."

"Shit, Jessup's just about the best crank chef these Dollys and them ever have had, girl. Practically half famous for it. That's why he pulled them years away up in the pen, there, you know. It was sure 'nough proved on him *that* time."

"That was last time. You got to prove it on him *every* time."

"That won't be no hard thing to do. But this noise, this noise ain't even why I'm here. Why I'm here is, his court date is next week and I can't seem to turn him up."

"Maybe he sees you comin' and ducks."

"Maybe he does. That could be. But where you-all come into this is, he put this house, here, and those timber acres up for his bond."

"He *what,* now?"

"Signed it all over. You didn't know? Jessup signed over everything. If he don't show for trial, see, the way the deal works is, you-all lose this place. It'll get sold from under you. You'll have to get out. Got somewhere to go?"

Ree nearly fell but would not let it happen in front of the law. She heard thunder clapping between her ears and Beelzebub scratchin' a fiddle. The boys and her and Mom would be dogs in the fields without this house. They would be dogs in the fields with Beelzebub scratchin' out tunes and the boys'd have a hard hard shove toward unrelenting meanness and the roasting shed and she'd be stuck alongside them 'til steel doors clanged shut and the flames rose. She'd never get away from her family as planned, off to the U.S. Army, where you got to travel with a gun and they made everybody help keep things clean. She'd never have only her own concerns to tote. She'd never have her own concerns.

Ree stretched over the rail, pulled her hair aside and let snow land on her neck. She closed her eyes, tried to call to mind the sounds of a far tranquil ocean, the lapping of waves. She said, "I'll find him."

"Girl, I been lookin', and . . ."

"*I'll find him.*"

Baskin waited a moment for another word to be spoken, then shook his head and walked to the top step, turned to look at her again, shrugged and started down. Dollys lugging meat paused to watch him, openly staring. Blond Milton, Sonya, Catfish Milton, Betsy and the rest. He waved to them and none moved a twitch in response. He said, "That'd be the best thing, girl. Make sure your daddy gets the gravity of this deal."

NEAR DUSK the snow let up. The wood of the house tightened in the cold and creaked and both boys had scratchy throats. Their chests jumped pumping out coughs. They had sniffles and voices becoming froggy from sickness. Ree sat them on couch cushions laid beside the potbelly, under the hanging clothes, and threw a quilt over them.

"I told the both of you to put your goddam stocking hats on, didn't I? Didn't I say that?"

Mom's evening pills did not tamp her as far down inside herself as the morning pills did. She did not stumble so wretchedly after concepts that squirted away from her time and again, but had occasional evening thoughts come complete and sit on her tongue to be said, and as the sun faded from a day she might release a few sentences of helpful chat or even lend a hand in the kitchen. She said, "There's whiskey hid in a ol' boot on my closet floor. Any honey anywhere?"

The whiskey was Jessup's, kept hidden from the boys, and Ree fetched it from the old boot. She had to stand on a chair to find a long-forgotten honey jar on a high shelf. The jar held an inch or two of crystallizing honey. She poured whiskey on the honey, then said, "This enough?"

"A dollop more. Stir it good."

Ree stirred with a tablespoon until the crystals dissolved in bourbon, then raised a gob and held it to Sonny's mouth.

"Swallow. All of it."

Then came Harold's turn, and as he swallowed somebody knocked on the door. Ree glanced at Mom, who got up from her rocker and shuffled away into her dark room without turning on a light. Ree went to the door and opened it with her boot wedged behind as a stopper should a stopper be needed.

"Oh. Hey, Sonya. Come in, why not."

Sonya carried a large cardboard box that had venison on a long bone jutting above the rim. Sonya was heavy and round, with gray hair and fogged glasses. She had four children grown and gone and a husband who still looked good to plenty of gals in these hills and knew it, so she could never banish suspicion from her face. Blond Milton stood fairly high amongst the Dollys and Ree knew he'd shared some hours on the sly with Mom years back, hurtful hours that Sonya had yet to forgive.

"Didn't want you-all to fear we'd forgot you for good." Sonya set the box on a chair. She clasped her hands and peered into the shadows of the house, noted the mess. Her nose wrinkled, her brows arched. There was a snap sermon said in the way she held her hands clasped against her bosom. "Got meat for you. Canned stuff. Some butter and such."

"We can use it."

"How's your mom gettin' to be?"

"Not better."

The laundry hung dry and the boys coughed.

"You poor thing. I'll have Betsy's Milton haul across a rick of wood for you-all. Looks like your pile's burned low. We seen the law was over here talkin' to you this after."

"He's huntin' for Dad. Dad's got a court day next week."

"Huntin' Jessup, is he?" Sonya lowered her glasses and looked up at Ree. "You know where he's at?"

"No."

"No? Well. Well, then, you didn't have nothin' to tell him. Did you?"

"Wouldn't never tell if I did."

"Oh, we know that." Sonya turned to the door, opened it on the cold night, paused. "If Jessup's court day ain't 'til next week, I kind of wonder why was the law out huntin' him for a talk *today?* Wonder why that would be."

Sonya did not wait for a response, but spun outside while pulling the door shut and quickly descended the steps. Ree stared from a window until Sonya reached the narrow foot-bridge and crossed the creek. She picked up the box. Her arms went around it and her hands locked. Good smells long lost to this kitchen returned with the box and spread as she carried it to the counter. Sonny and Harold hacked, sniffed, snorted, but shot up together from beneath the quilt and rushed to the food. They opened sacks, hefted cans, kept croaking, "Oh, boy, oh, boy."

Ree saw four days inside that box. Four days free from hunger or worrying about hunger returning at daybreak, maybe five. She said, "I'll be fixin' deer stew tonight. That sound good? Both of you two need to watch how I make it. Hear me? I mean it. Haul them chairs over here and stand on 'em with your eyes peeled and watch every goddam thing I do. Learn how I make it, then you both'll know."

S HE'D START with Uncle Teardrop, though Uncle Teardrop scared her. He lived three miles down the creek but she walked on the railroad tracks. Snow covered the tracks and made humps over the rails and the twin humps guided her. She broke her own trail through the snow and booted the miles from her path. The morning sky was gray and crouching, the wind had snap and drew water to her eyes. She wore a green hooded sweatshirt and Mamaw's black coat. Ree nearly always wore a dress or skirt, but with combat boots, and the skirt this day was a bluish plaid. Her knees kicked free of the plaid when she threw her long legs forward and stomped the snow.

The world seemed huddled and hushed and her crunching steps cracked loud as ax whacks. As she crunched past houses built on yon slopes yard dogs barked faintly from under porches but none came into the cold to make a run at her and flash teeth. Smoke poured from every chimney and was promptly flattened east by the wind. There was deer sign trod below trestles that stood over the creek and thin ice clung around rocks in the shallows. Where the creek forked she left the tracks and walked uphill through deeper snow beside an old pioneer fencerow made of piled stones.

Uncle Teardrop's place sat beyond one daunting ridge and up a narrow draw. The house had been built small but extra bedrooms and box windows and other ideas had been added on by different residents who'd had hammers and leftover wood. There always seemed to be walls covered by black tarpaper standing alone for months and months waiting for more walls and a roof to come along and complete a room. Stovepipes angled from the house on every which side.

Three dogs that were a mess of hunting breeds lived under the big screened deck. Ree had known them since they were pups and called out as she reached the yard and they came to sniff her nethers and wag welcome. They barked, jumped, and slapped tongues at her until Victoria opened the main door.

She said, "Somebody dead?"

"Not that I heard."

"You walked over in this nasty crud just for a visit, dear? You must be purty awful lonely."

"I'm lookin' for Dad. I got to run him down, and quick."

That certain women who did not seem desperate or crazy could be so deeply attracted to Uncle Teardrop confused and frightened Ree. He was a nightmare to look at but he'd torn through a fistful of appealing wives. Victoria had once been number three and was now number five. She was a tall blunt-boned woman made lush in her sections with long auburn hair she usually wore rolled up into a heavy wobbly bun. She had a closet that held no jeans or slacks but was stuffed with dresses old and new and most of Ree's things had first been worn by her. In winter Victoria was given to reading gardening books and seed catalogues and at spring planting she disdained the commonplace Big Boy or Early Girl tomatoes in favor of exotic international strains she got by mail and doted on and always tasted like a mouthful of far pretty lands.

"Well, then, come on in, kiddo. Shake off the chill. Jessup ain't here, but coffee's hot." Victoria held the door for Ree. Victoria smelled wonderful up close, like she always did, some scent she had that when smelled went into the blood like dope and left you near woozy. She looked good and smelled good and Ree favored her over any other Dolly woman but Mom. "Teardrop mightn't be up yet, so let's keep it down 'til he is."

They sat at the eating table. A skylight had been cut into the ceiling and leaked rainwater from the low corners sometimes but helped a lot to brighten the room. Ree could see through the house to the front door and over to the rear door and noted that a long gun stood ready beside both. A silver pistol and clip rested in a nut bowl on the lazy Susan centered upon the table. Beside the pistol there was a big bag of pot and a pretty big bag of crank.

Victoria said, "Ree, I forget — you take it black, or with cream?"

"With cream when there is any."

"Ain't that the truth."

They hunched over the table and sipped. A cuckoo clock chirped nine times. Record albums lined along the floor went nearly the complete length of a wall. There was a fancy-looking sound system on a bookshelf, plus a four-foot rack of CDs. The furniture was mostly wooden, country-type stuff. One piece was a big round cushioned chair on a sapling frame that you sat in the exact middle of like you were squatted inside a bloomed flower. Swirly-patterned lavender cloth from Arabia was tacked to a wall as decoration.

"The law came by. That Baskin one. He said if Dad don't show for his court day next week we got to move out of the house. Dad signed it over to go his bond. They'll take the place from us. And the timber acres, too. Victoria, I *really, really* got to run Dad to ground and get him to show."

Uncle Teardrop stood stretching in the bedroom doorway and said, "You ought not do that." He wore a white T-shirt and plum sweatpants stuffed into untied boots. He was a nudge over six feet tall but had fidgeted his weight way down and become all muscle wires and bone knobs with a sunken belly. "Don't go runnin' after Jessup." Teardrop sat at the table. "Coffee." He rapped his fingers to the tabletop and made a hoofbeat rhythm. "What's this shit all about, anyhow?"

"I got to find Dad'n make sure he shows in court."

"That's a man's personal choice, little girl. That's not somethin' you oughta be buttin' your smarty nose into. Show or don't show, that choice is up to the one that's goin' to jail to make. Not you."

Uncle Teardrop was Jessup's elder and had been a crank chef longer but he'd had a lab go wrong and it had eaten the left ear off his head and burned a savage melted scar down his neck to the middle of his back. There wasn't enough ear nub remaining to hang sunglasses on. The hair around the ear was gone, too, and the scar on his neck showed above his collar. Three blue teardrops done in jailhouse ink fell in a row from the corner of the eye on his scarred side. Folks said the teardrops meant he'd three times done grisly prison deeds that needed doing but didn't need to be gabbed about. They said the teardrops told you everything you had to know about the man and the lost ear just repeated it. He generally tried to sit with his melted side to the wall.

Ree said, "Come on, you know where he's at, don't you?"

"And where a man's at ain't necessarily for you to know, neither."

"But, do you—"

"Ain't seen him."

Teardrop stared at Ree with a flat expression of finality and Victoria jumped in between them, asking, "How's your mom?"

Ree tried to hold Teardrop's gaze but blinked uncontrollably. It was like staring at something fanged and coiled from too close without a stick in hand.

"Not better."

"And the boys?"

Ree broke and looked down, scared and slumping.

"A little pindlin' but not pukey sick," she said. She looked to her lap and her clenched hands and drove her fingernails into her palms, gouging fiercely, raising pink crescents on her milk skin, then turned toward Uncle Teardrop and leaned desperately his way. "Could he be runnin' with Little Arthur and them again? You think? That bunch from Hawkfall? Should I look for him around there?"

Teardrop raised his hand and drew it back to smack her and

let fly but diverted the smacking hand inches from Ree's face to the nut bowl. His fingers dove rattling into the nuts, beneath the silver pistol, and lifted it from the lazy Susan. He bounced the weapon on his flat palm as though judging the weight with his hand for a scale, sighed, then ran a finger gently along the barrel to brush away grains of salt.

"Don't you, nor nobody else, neither, *ever* go down around Hawkfall askin' them people shit about stuff they ain't *offerin'* to talk about. That's a real good way to end up et by hogs, or wishin' you was. You ain't no silly-assed town girl. You know better'n that foolishness."

"But we're all related, ain't we?"

"Our relations get watered kinda thin between this valley here and Hawkfall. It's better'n bein' a foreigner or town people, but it ain't nowhere near the same as bein' *from* Hawkfall."

Victoria said, "You know all those people down there, Teardrop. You could ask."

"Shut up."

"I just mean, none of them's goin' to be in a great big hurry to tangle with you, neither. If Jessup's over there, Ree needs to see him. *Bad.*"

"I said shut up once already, with my mouth."

Ree felt bogged and forlorn, doomed to a spreading swamp of hateful obligations. There would be no ready fix or answer or help. She felt like crying but wouldn't. She could be beat with a garden rake and never cry and had proved that twice before Mamaw saw an unsmiling angel pointing from the treetops at dusk and quit the bottle. She would never cry where her tears might be seen and counted against her. "Jesus-fuckin'-Christ, Dad's your *only* little brother!"

"You think I forgot that?" He grabbed the clip and slammed it into the pistol, then ejected it and tossed pistol and clip back into the nut bowl. He made a fist with his right hand and rubbed it with his left. "Jessup'n me run together for nigh on forty years — but I *don't know* where he's at, and I ain't goin' to go around askin' after him, neither."

Ree knew better than to say another word, but was going to anyhow, when Victoria grabbed her hand and held it, squeezed, then said, "Now, *when is it* you was tellin' me you'll be old enough to join the army?"

"Next birthday."

"Then you'll be off from here?"

"I hope."

"Good for you. Good deal. But, what'll the boys and —"

Teardrop lurched from his chair and snatched Ree by the hair and pulled her head hard his way and yanked back so her throat was bared and her face pointed up. He ran his eyes into her like a serpent down a hole, made her feel his slither in her heart and guts, made her tremble. He jerked her head one way and another, then pressed a hand around her windpipe and held her still. He leaned his face to hers from above and nuzzled his melt against her cheek, nuzzled up and down, then slid his lips to her forehead, kissed her once and let go. He picked up the crank bag from the lazy Susan. He held it toward the skylight and shook the bag while looking closely at the shifting powder. He carried the bag toward the bedroom and Victoria motioned Ree to sit still, then slowly followed him. She pulled the door shut and whispered something. A talk with two voices started low and calm but soon one voice raised alone and spoke several tart muffled sentences. Ree could not follow any words through the wall. There was a lull of silence more uncomfortable than the tart sentences had been. Victoria came back, head lowered, blowing her nose into a pale blue tissue.

"Teardrop says you best keep your ass real close to the willows, dear." She dropped fifty dollars in tens on the tabletop and fanned the bills. "He hopes this helps. Want me to roll a doobie for your walk?"

SHE TOOK to pausing more often to study on things that weren't usually of interest. She sniffed the air like it might somehow have changed flavors and looked closely at the stone fencerow, touched the stones and hefted a few, held them to her face, saw a rabbit that didn't try to run until she laughed at it, smelled Victoria on her sleeves and hunkered atop a stump to think. She spread her skirt taut across her knees and tucked the extra under her legs. Those stones had probably been piled by direct ancestors and for a long while she tried to conjure their pioneer lives and think if she saw parts of their lives showing in her own. With her eyes closed she could call them near, see those olden Dolly kin who had so many bones that broke, broke and mended, broke and mended wrong, so they limped through life on the bad-mend bones for year upon year until falling dead in a single evening from something that sounded wet in the lungs. The men came to mind as mostly idle between nights of running wild or time in the pen, cooking moon and gathering around the spout, with ears chewed, fingers chopped, arms shot away, and no apologies grunted ever. The women came to mind bigger, closer, with their lonely eyes and homely yellow teeth, mouths clamped against smiles, working in the hot fields from can to can't, hands tattered rough as dry cobs, lips cracked all winter, a white dress for marrying, a black dress for burying, and Ree nodded yup. Yup.

The sky lay dark and low so a hawk circling overhead floated in and out of clouds. The wind heaved and knocked the hood from her head. That hawk was riding the heaving wind looking to kill something. Looking to snatch something, rip it bloody, chew the tasty parts, let the bones drop.

Dad could be anywhere.

Dad might think he had reasons to be most anywhere or do most anything, even if the reasons seemed ridiculous in the morning.

One night when Ree was still a bantling Dad had gotten crossways with Buster Leroy Dolly and been shot in the chest clear out by Twin Forks River. He was electric on crank, thrilled to have been shot, and instead of driving to a doctor he drove thirty miles to West Table and the Tiny Spot Tavern to show his assembled buddies the glamorous bullet hole and the blood bubbling. He collapsed grinning and the drunks carried him to the town hospital and nobody thought he'd live to see noon until he did.

Dad was tough enough but not much on planning. At eighteen he'd left the Ozarks planning to work for big dough on the oil rigs of Louisiana but ended up boxing Mexicans for peanuts in Texas. He slugged them, they slugged him, everybody bled, nobody got rich. Three years later he came back to the valley with nothing to show for his adventure but new scars ragged around both eyes and a few stories men chuckled at for a while.

Dad could be anywhere with anybody.

Mom's mind didn't break loose and scatter to the high weeds until Ree was twelve and around then is when she learned about Dad's girlfriend. Her name was Dunahew and she taught kindergarten down across the Arkansas line at Reid's Gap. Her front name was April and she wasn't so hot to look at but she had sweet fat ways and a steady paycheck. Ree had once been taken to Reid's Gap and left there for most of a week to nurse April through a sickness in her stomach. That was two years ago and she'd not heard Dad say April's name since or smelled her on his clothes. April owned a pretty yellow house just west of the main road down there, and Dad could be anywhere.

HALFWAY BETWEEN Uncle Teardrop's and home Ree turned west on the creek road and climbed a snowy ridge, crossed a white meadow. The Langans had a single-wide trailer that was tan and sat on a concrete pad behind their junk barn. The barn was made of wood that had been drenched by generations of weather and rendered gray and rickety. It tilted one way near the front and another near the back. Junk items unlikely to be needed ever again were tossed into the barn and forgotten. The single-wide had a raised deck and men could piss from a corner to the side of the barn and a short frayed shadow of discoloration had been splattered there.

Gail Lockrum, Ree's best friend, had been required by pregnancy to marry Floyd Langan and now lived in the tan single-wide next to his parents. Gail and Ree had been tight since the second-grade field trip when they'd bumped heads chasing the same frog under a picnic table at Mammoth Spring and stood to rub their ouches, then took a shine to each other and since spent the idle hours of each passing year happily swapping clothes and dreams and their opinions of everybody else. Gail had a baby named Ned who was four months old, and a new look of baffled hurt, a left-behind sadness, like she saw that the great world kept spinning onward and away while she'd overnight become glued to her spot.

Ree heard Ned squalling as she stepped onto the deck. She stood a moment in snow crust, paused at the door, then knocked. There was the slam of a La-Z-Boy footrest being lowered, mutters. The door seemed stuck by ice and had to be bullied open, and when it was Gail stood there holding Ned, and said, "Thank god it's you, Sweet Pea, and not Floyd's goddam mommy'n daddy again. Them two watch me like I done somethin' wrong or at least maybe I'm fixin' to the first day they *ain't* watchin' me."

Floyd said, "Would you hush your mouth about them? Just stick a pickle in it. They put a roof over your head, ain't they?"

Ree smiled and reached to pinch Ned's little cheek but recoiled from his demanding mottle-faced squalling and dropped her hand. She looked at his baby face all scrunched up sour by wants he'd been born bawling for but might never be able to name or get for himself, and said, "You goin' to ask me in, or do I gotta stand out here?"

Floyd said, "She can come in. For a little."

Gail said, "Hear that?"

"Yup."

Floyd sat in the front room of the trailer, lying back in his chair, holding a snow-day beer, headphones on a long cord resting in his lap. He was almost twenty and Ree knew most girls would call him handsome or dreamy or some such.

Sandy hair, blue eyes, put together strong, with bright teeth and one of those smiles. He'd been steady in love with Heather Powney since junior high but once when Heather was away he'd gotten drunk and come across Gail at the Sonic in town and sat with her in his car listening to thrash metal while the windows fogged. He saw Gail the next night, too, but that was it until Old Man Lockrum came over months later redassed and huffing. Suddenly Floyd became a husband with a kid and Heather Powney didn't always take his calls anymore.

Ree said, "Hey, Floyd — been gettin' any?"

"Nope. Learned my lesson on that." He raised the headphones and held them spread near his ears. "Don't hang around too long. She's got that kid now."

"Yeah, I noticed him."

Floyd let the headphones snap closed and waved her away.

Gail stood in the kitchen with Ned held to her chest. Gail was thin in the hips and limbs with sharp smart features and freckles. Her long hair fell straight and was of a ruddled hue matched to the freckles dusted across her nose and cheeks. Somehow her skinny body had hid the baby behind a merely rounding tummy and she'd looked more pooched than pregnant until her seventh month. She never did get waddling pregnant and had been skinny again within a few weeks of delivery. She still seemed stunned by this sudden wife-and-mother business and disbelieving that it mightn't all go away as quickly as it'd come.

Ree smelled the grease leavings in the skillet and the cloth diapers soaking in the washtub. She saw plates gunky in the sink and pork for tonight thawing pink trickles on the side-board. She threw her arms around Gail with the baby between and kissed Gail's cheek, her nose, her other cheek. She said, "Aw, Sweet Pea, shit."

"Don't start. Don't start."

Ree brushed her fingers into Gail's hair, pulled the long strands apart and picked between them, picked gently and many times.

"Sweet Pea, you got sticky-burrs."

"Still?"

"I sure keep findin' 'em."

The baby was taking a moment to rest and slobber between outbursts and Gail hefted him along the narrow hall-way to the main bedroom while Ree followed. Big posters of race cars shiny inside shrinkwrap were taped to the walls. A giant beer mug filled brown with pennies sat on the dresser. The bed was an unmade wallow of yellow sheets and patch-work blankets. Gail laid Ned on the bed, then sat beside him and said, "Been a while, Sweet Pea." She fell stretched back-wards beside the baby with her arms flopped wide and her feet on the floor. "It's like I make you too sad for you to come see me."

"That's only part of why."

"What's the rest?"

"Things stack up, is all."

"So talk to me."

Ree sat on a stick chair and lifted Gail's feet to her lap. She hunched over with her eyes down, rubbed her hands along Gail's calves and ankles, all the while telling of Dad and the law, Dad and the house, her and the boys and Beelzebub's fiddle. The light in the window passed from dim to gloomy and back to dim while Floyd now and then raised his voice to join the chorus in his headphones and drone thrash lyrics unattached to music behind Ree's words. She rubbed with bracing vigor until she'd said enough.

"Reid's Gap? Where exactly's that?"

"Past Dorta, on the Arkansas side. She's a kindy-garden teacher."

"I got to ask him. He keeps the keys."

"Tell him I can spring for gas."

Gail rolled from the bed, fell to her feet, and walked toward the droning voice. She was gone but a moment. When she came back to Ree, she said, "He won't let me drive."

"You tell him I'll spring for gas?"

"I told him. He still won't."

"Why not?"

"He never says why not to me. He just says no."

"Aw, Sweet Pea." Ree shook her head. The features of her face seemed to curdle together. "I hate that."

"What? What's so awful wrong to make that face?"

"It's just so sad, man, so fuckin' sad to hear you say he won't let you do somethin', and then you *don't* do it."

Gail fell stiff like a tree limb to the bed, crashed her face flat into the sheets.

"It's different once you're married."

"Must be. Must really be. You never used to eat no shit. No shit at all."

Gail turned and spun to sit on the edge of the bed. Ned

gurgled, churned the air with tiny clenched hands. Gail's head sagged and Ree leaned to pick at her hair, pinched between the long ruddled locks, brushed strands back with her fingertips, lowered her face and inhaled the smell.

Gail said in a low voice, "What're you doin'?"

"Pluckin' sticky-burrs, darlin'. You got a mess of sticky-burrs."

"No, I don't." She pushed Ree's hands away but did not raise her eyes. "I don't got sticky-burrs. And Ned'n me need our nap. I feel tired of a sudden. We'll see you next time, Sweet Pea."

Ree slowly stood in the dimness, kicked a boot against the stick chair, pulled the green hood up around her head, then said, "Just, I'm *always* for you, remember."

When Ree came out the front door Floyd stood at the corner of the deck lashing an arc of piss to the junk barn wall. The piss hit the wall and steamed, steamed and bubbled brief suds sliding down the wall to the snowbank. Hot drops burrowed into the snow and left jaundiced dots and scrawls. He continued to piss, shivering in shirtsleeves, shoulders hunched against the breeze, and said, "Reckon it'll ever turn cold today?"

"If it don't today it will tonight."

Steam rose from the barn wall in light wisps and Floyd glanced over his shoulder at Ree. He said, "You think you get it but you don't. I mean, you oughta try it your own self sometime. Get drunk one night and wind up married to somebody you don't hardly know."

"I know her real good."

"Yes'm, girl, you oughta go'n get yourself good'n drunk one night and have you a kid. I mean it."

"No thanks. I already got two. Not countin' Mom."

Floyd's arc of piss slackened and slackened until he shook the last drops loose.

"Nobody here wants to be awful," he said. He hopped a little as he zipped up. "It's just nobody here knows all the rules yet, and that makes a rocky time."

REE FOLLOWED a path made by prey uphill through scrub, across a bald knob and downhill into a section of pine trees and pine scent and that pious shade and silence pines create. Pine trees with low limbs spread over fresh snow made a stronger vault for the spirit than pews and pulpits ever could. She lingered. She sat on a big thinking rock amid the pines and clamped her headphones on. She tried to match the imported sounds to the setting and selected *Alpine Dusk*. But those wintry mountain sounds matched the view too perfectly and she switched to *The Sounds of Tropical Dawn*. Snow worked loose on branches overhead and sifted between pine needles to drift down as powder while she heard warm waves unrolling and birds of many colors and maybe monkeys. She could hear the smell of orchids and papayas, sense a rainbow of fish gathering in the shallows near the beach.

She sat there until the big thinking rock made her butt too cold.

GRAY NAILED down over the sky complete and all the windows. Mom's head bent into the kitchen sink and her hair billowed to fill the basin. She seemed lost to an episode of splendid pleasure, given up entirely to the joys of being fussed over by a daughter, mewling as Ree's fingers scrubbed her scalp, raised a shock of white lather, rinsed with water poured from Mamaw's ancient lemonade pitcher. Ree's fingers were strong and drew blood tingling to the roots. The boys sat on the countertop close enough to be splashed, wrapped in quilts, watching her scrub, lather, rinse. Ree glanced their way frequently to keep their attention. She'd nod toward Mom's head in a gesture that asked, Are you getting this?

Harold said, "Some suds got missed."

"We'll get 'em with the next rinse."

Sonny called forth a shallow cough and said, "Got'ny more of that syrup?"

"Huh-uh. You two like it too much."

"It sure gets rid of that scratchy feelin' good, though."

Ice hung from the roof eaves, catching dribbles of melt to become longer and stouter pickets of jagged freeze stretched across the window above the sink. The sun was weak in the west, a faint smudge behind middling clouds, and low. Soup stock from deer bones simmered on the stove and steamed a comforting scent.

"Might could mix you some later — but now you watch this. Watch how to do her hair."

Harold said, "Got suds in her ear still."

"Forget them goddam suds — watch what I'm showin' you. So, now, once the soap is good'n washed out you're s'posed to dump conditioner on, but alls we got handy is vinegar. So we'll use vinegar. Watch close how I measure this out."

The television competed for the boys' attention. This deep in the valley reception was poor and they only received two channels, but the public channel from Arkansas came in best and the late-afternoon shows the boys loved were about to commence. The smiley dog that jumped around among time periods chasing adventure and historical insight came on the screen wearing a suit of shining armor. As the vinegar smell spread and Ree bent over Mom yet again, both boys quietly slid from the counter and made for the front room and the worldly dog.

Ree watched them go.

"You're about to look peachy, Mom."

"Could I?"

"Yup. So peachy you'll be feelin' all strutty, probly start dancin', kick your toes to the ceilin'."

"Could I?"

"You used to."

"That's true, isn't it? I did used to."

"Was special to see when you did, too."

Ree gripped Mom's hind hair like a rope and squeezed, squeezed and twisted. The last free drops twisted loose to run down Ree's hand and wrist and she dried on a towel. She then spread the towel over the pile of wet hair.

"Sit by the stove so I can comb you out and get you dry."

There was a perimeter of warmth around the potbelly and Mom sat with her head held straight. Ree took a wide-tooth comb to the hair, raked it back into a jumbo sleekness, patted it with the towel, then slicked it again. When Dad was in the pen Mom'd dolled up a lot, every weekend night, dressed herself sparkly hot and let herself be taken places. Her eyes would shine and she'd act girlish while she waited, then a horn would honk and she'd say, "I'll be back, babe. Have fun."

She'd be back for breakfast looking worn, jaded and uneasy. Shaking the ache of loneliness is what she slipped away into those smoky nights hoping to do, but she never could shake it from her trail. It was always back in her eyes by breakfast. Sometimes marks showed and Ree'd ask who did that and she'd answer, "A beau did, sayin' good-bye."

"You smell nice, Mom."

"Like flowers?"

"Some kind probly."

Came a time when Mom told Ree details about those nights out in roadhouse joints, or parties at the East Main Trailer Court, or how things got out of hand at the River Bluff Motel. The time of telling came when Mom sensed the smoky nights were done for her and she'd taken to fingering the memories of them from her rocking chair. She'd absorbed a few beatings for love in life and gotten over them, but it was those terrible ass-whippings she'd taken during one-night stands, motel quickies with fellas from the Bar Circle Z Ranch or handsome tramps in town that hung with her. Those times just hung in the mind swaying, swaying, casting shadows behind her eyes forever. Love and hate hold hands always so it made natural sense that they'd get confused by upset married folk in the wee hours once in a while and a nosebleed or bruised breast might result. But it just seemed proof that a great foulness was afoot in the world when a no-strings roll in the hay with a stranger led to chipped teeth or cigarette burns on the wrist.

"I think I'll root around and find your makeup, too. Get you painted up special today."

"Like before was."

"A lot of the time."

But there'd been hot buttered parts of those nights she'd liked so and missed. The sweet beginnings that held the promise of who knows what, the scent, the music, the shouted names in a loud place, names you might never get straight. The spark of fun when two men quickened at the sight of her, stepped forward on the same snap and tried to woo her, one in this ear, the other in that. Lust slaking to dance tunes, standing hip bone to hip bone, the new hands moving over her rumples and furls and tender knobs, hands good as tongues in the dark corners of those whiskey moments. Words were the hungered-for need, and the necessary words would be spoken low, sometimes sounding so truly true she could believe them with all her heart until the naked gasp happened and the man started looking for his boots on the floor. That moment always drained her of belief in the words and the man, or any words and any man.

"Don't fidget — you're near about dry."

While Dad was in prison the rule had been to never see the same stud three nights. One night is forgot like a fart, two like a pang, but after three nights lain together there is a hurt, and to soothe the hurt there will be night four, and five, and nights unnumbered. The heart's in it then, spinning dreams, and torment is on the way. The heart makes dreams seem like ideas.

Ree went into Mom's room and flicked on the light. The walls were papered pink from Mamaw's day. There was a nice curly maple dresser with a mirror that had been Aunt Bernadette's before the flash flood caught her dawdling strangely on the low bridge and never even gave her body back. Hard not to see glimpses of her face in the creek or the mirror since. Above the bed there was a dusty, cockeyed picture of Uncle Jack, who'd lived through Khe Sanh and four marriages, then died at a roller-skating rink from something he'd snorted. The bed had brass parts, fat brass tubes at the head and the foot, and the bedspread was red and kicked aside. Ree'd been made in that bed, and she'd caught Mom and Blond Milton making Sonny there on a slow sweaty morning. Mom'd already begun to crack in her senses a little and flung an ashtray at Ree, shouting, "You're lyin'! You're lyin'! This could never happen!"

"Can't find your makeup kit, Mom. I'll paint your face pretty another time."

Mom rocked in warmth beside the potbelly, touching her hands to her hair, and did not seem to have heard. She stared across the kitchen toward the television, squinted past her two sons and cocked her head sideways.

"Wonder where'd he get that armor from?"

COYOTES HOWLED past dawn, howled from far crags and ridges and down the valley to the end of the rut road where the school bus stopped. Ree, Sonny, and Harold stood next to the county blacktop that led everywhere, beside white levees the plows had built with scraped-aside snow. The morning was clear but bone-cracking cold, and maybe the weather had kept those coyotes from doing what had to be done in the night so they carried on into the day. Wild crooning yips and moans beneath a sun that warmed nothing. Ree kept the boys huddled close together, watched the breath spewing from their mouths like those little clouds that carried words of thought in cartoons. Harold's cloud might say, "Hope they don't eat people much." And Sonny's, "Got'ny more of that syrup?"

The Junction School sat six miles distant, next to the main road that led to West Table. The bus was like a big bus but cut short, not half the size. It was yellow with black warnings painted front and back and carried maybe a dozen or a few more kids each day. It stopped at rut roads, skinny rock lanes, certain open spaces between trees. A lot of the kids were cousins to some vague degree, but that didn't keep them from roughhousing, name-calling, and all the rest. A couple times a week it seemed the bus ride got out of control and Mr. Egan would pull over and swat somebody.

Harold said, "Could be we should set food out, Ree."

"For them coyotes? Nah. Don't fret. Not much chance they'll eat you."

"Wouldn't be no chance if we set food out."

Sonny said, "Just shoot 'em. They come sniffin' close, just shoot 'em 'tween the eyes."

"But they look like dogs," Harold said. "Dogs are okay by me even if they're hungry."

Ree said, "Settin' out food'll draw 'em close — that's likely how they'll come too close and get shot, Harold. Don't set no goddam food out. It looks like you're doin' nice, but you ain't. You're just bringin' 'em into range, is all."

"But you can hear how hungry they are."

The bus broke the horizon above the next ridge and rolled downhill toward them faster on the blacktop than looked safe. Mr. Egan stopped beside them, flipped the door open, said, "Quick. Quick."

The boys stepped up and got on and Ree followed.

"Can I ride today?"

Mr. Egan was about fifty years old, a settling heap of flesh with extra chins loose below heavy gray face stubble and thin pale hair. He had a bad leg, a leg he had to drag, and when asked about it he'd say, "If ol' Four-Eyes Orrick ever up'n asks you to go jackin' deer with him, *don't go.*" He smiled at Ree and pulled the door closed.

"Startin' back to school?"

"Nope. I could just use a ride."

"Okey-doke. I miss havin' you on here."

"You do?"

"Yup. Damn near quit drivin' when you quit ridin'."

"Applesauce."

"No applesauce, princess. There just about ain't no sunshine when you're gone."

Ree sat behind Mr. Egan. She grinned at the boys across the aisle. She pointed a finger at her head and made circles near her ear. The bus lunged along the blacktop at a good clip. She said, "Are you hopin' to get in my britches, man?"

"Don't be disgustin', Ree."

"Oh. Kind of sorry to hear you say it all final that way."

"I've hauled you since you were six years old." The bus rushed past the forest so fast the woods seemed to be streaming. The long morning shadows from the tall trees spoked the light to spin vision from dark to bright, dark to bright, dazzling the eyes on the bus. "I'm a happily divorced man with a shaky pump. Don't tease me all around tryin' to mix me up."

"Okay, but thanks, though."

"Well, princess, I know damn well how just about everywhere is too far to walk to from out here."

The school area consisted of two buildings and both resembled automobile-repair garages of a giant sort, prefab metal sheds divided into several classrooms and offices. The larger shed was the Junction School, painted off-white with a black roof, and it held the grades below high school. The Rathlin Valley High School sat across the schoolyard, with its own parking lot, and had russet walls with a white roof. The sports name for all grades was the Fighting Bobcats, and a large picture of several toothy cats with extended claws raking red slashes into a blue sky was painted on a billboard set beside the blacktop. The bus stopped next to the other buses just past the billboard.

Ree said, "Don't fight if you can help it. But if one of you gets whipped by somebody *both* of you best come home bloody, understand?"

Ree crossed the schoolyard snow toward the scraped hard road that led north. She saw pregnant girls she knew huddled by their special side entrance holding textbooks and bumping bellies. She saw boys she knew sharing smoke, crouched beside their pickup trucks. She saw lovers she knew kissing back and forth with enough wet kisses to hold each sated and faithful until the lunch hour. She saw teachers she knew watching with sad eyes as she left the schoolyard alone to stand beside the north road with her thumb out. She waved once to Mrs. Prothero and Mr. Feltz, but wouldn't look toward the school again.

The landscape of freeze framed her so pitifully that she had a lift within minutes. A Schwan's food delivery truck stopped for her, and the driver said several times he wasn't supposed to give rides but, jeez, that wind, that wind sort of blows the rules away, don't it? He carried her past the ramshackle wide spots of Bawbee, Heaney Cross and Chaunk, past the turn to Haslam Springs, and on to the y-fork above Hawkfall. His route and hers split there, and Ree climbed down and watched the truck drive away north.

The Hawkfall road had not been plowed below the crest. Ree came down the great steep hill, walking in the lone set of swerving wheel ruts pressed into the snow. The houses of the village sat in the bottomland and perched low or high on surrounding slopes and ridges. The new part of Hawkfall was old to most folks, but the old part of Hawkfall seemed ancient and a creepy sort of sacred. The old and new places had mainly been made of Ozark stone. The walls of the old places had been pulled apart, the stones torn asunder and tossed furiously about the meadow during the bitter reckoning of long ago. The stones had ever since been left lay where they fell and now raised scattered white humps across three acres. The new places had smoke churning from chimneys and footprints in their yards.

Keening blue wind was bringing weather back into the sky, dark clouds gathering at the edge of sight, carrying frosty wet for later. A fat brown dog came waddling through tummy-deep snow to investigate Ree, sniffed and barked his findings until three more dogs came springing across the road to bounce around her. She was escorted by frisky mutts as she walked past the meadow of the old fallen walls and into the village. The low stone houses had short front porches and tall skinny windows. Most places still had two front doors in accordance with certain readings of Scripture, one door for men, the other for women, though nobody much used them strictly that way anymore. At the first house a woman came out the man door onto the porch and said, "Who're you?"

Ree stood on the road in a drift that touched her knees. "My name's Dolly. I'm a Dolly. Ree Dolly."

The woman was young, maybe twenty-five, wearing a tie-dyed bathrobe over a gray fuzzy sweater, black jeans, and boots. Her hair was nearly black, cut short and smart-looking, and she wore sort of burly eyeglasses that made smartness look cute on her. A stereo played behind her, a song with guitars strumming jangly and wild horses running free in the words. She said, "I don't guess I know you."

"I'm from Rathlin Valley? Down on Bromont Creek? You know where that is?"

"Might just about as well be Timbuktu to us," she said. "What's your business here?"

"My dad, Jessup, he's pals with Little Arthur, and I got to find him. I been here before. I know which house is where Little Arthur lives."

The woman lit a crooked yellow cigarette, flicked the match into the snow. She kept her eyes on Ree and her breath and the smoke spun white into the air. The dogs had climbed the steps to sniff her feet and she nudged them back with her boots. She said, "You stand right there 'til I get my hat. Don't go nosin' 'round anywhere."

Houses above looked caught on the scraggly hillsides like crumbs in a beard and apt to fall as suddenly. They'd been there two or three lifetimes, though, and cascades of snow, mushes of rain, and huffing spring wind had tried to knock them loose and send them tumbling but never did. There were narrow footpaths wending all about the slopes between the trees, along the rock ledges, from house to house, and in better weather Ree thought Hawkfall looked sort of enchanted, if a place could be enchanted but not too friendly. Up the road she saw tire tracks that left the hollow in the other direction. It was the long way to get to most useful places but there was no hill of snow to climb before the blacktop in that direction.

The woman came out the door and down from her porch, careful of the crusty steps, wearing a pearl-colored cowboy hat with a blue feather in the band. Her joint had smoked small and she held it to Ree, who took it and inhaled. The woman said, "I do know you, really. I seen you at some of the reunions at Rocky Drop."

"We don't always go."

"You one time smacked fire out the ass of a fat Boshell boy who flicked a booger on your dress, didn't you?"

"You *saw* that?"

"Knocked his plate of deviled eggs flyin', then made the boy say uncle with his mouth in the dirt. And you got the momma who went daffy in her head, too, right? Live close by Blond Milton out there?"

"Yup. That's all me."

"My name's Megan. And I knew Jessup when I seen him, too, but never did talk with him none."

"You *knew* him?"

Ree had smoked the joint down to scrap and held it to Megan. Megan popped it into her mouth and swallowed, then said, "Knew him when I seen him around, I mean. He does stuff I hear about."

"Oh. Well, he cooks crank."

"Honey, they all do now. You don't even need to say it out loud."

Ree and Megan began to walk toward Little Arthur's, boots squeaking into snow, and the dogs rallied about them, flicking tails against their shins, then bounding ahead to break the drifts. As they passed other houses folks opened their doors to look. Megan would wave to them and they'd wave back and the doors would close. The stone faces of the houses had caught snow in their burls and creases and looked like small ideal cliffs in the wild.

Little Arthur's place was up the slope, nearly to the top of the ridge. His house was built more of wood than stone but there was plenty of stone. On the steepest side of the house there had been a porch outside the kitchen door but the stairs and pilings had broken away to leave the floor unsupported above a hellish plummet, a beguiling bad idea lying in wait for somebody high to give it a try. Two bullet-riddled barrels and other metal debris rusted near the house and a battered beige car seat had been set against the wall as a summer bench. A silhouette moved in the front window as the women approached.

Megan said, "If he's been runnin' on crank for a day or two, you should just leave, honey. Don't try'n make sense to him when he's like that, 'cause he just can't do it behind that much shit."

"I know Little Arthur. He knows me. I got to find Dad."

The door opened and Little Arthur smiled at Ree and said, "I knew it — I been in your dreams, ain't I?"

"She's lookin' for Jessup — you seen him?"

"You mean she ain't lookin' for me? Ain't you really lookin' for *me,* Ruthie?"

"It's Ree, you asshole. And I'm only out to find Dad."

"Asshole? Hmmm. Now, I *like* a girl that calls me bad names, like her a lot, like her a whole precious bunch, right up 'til I don't like her none at all no more. That's always a weepy fuckin' time when that time happens." Little Arthur was a little-man mix of swagger and tongue, with a trailing history of deeds that vouched for his posture. He had a mess of dark hair and dark bristly eyes, with sparse curly whiskers and bitter teeth. Even without crank in his blood he always seemed cocked, poised to split in a flash from wherever he stood. He wore a couple of checked shirts, one tucked, one open, and a black pistol grip showed above his belt buckle. "Come in, ladies — or're you leavin', Meg?"

"Think maybe I'll stay a bit. Kind of cold."

"Suit yourself. Sit anywhere."

The house smelled of old beer, old grease, old smoke. No fresh light made it through the windows at this time of day and it was as shadowed as a sinkhole. The main room was long but narrow and a big square table had to be edged past to go from one side to the other. Pie pans had been used as ashtrays and sat full of butts on the table, the floor, both windowsills. A glistening pump shotgun lay broken open across the table.

Megan sat on an edge of the table and Little Arthur did the same. Ree skinnied past them to stand near a window and said, "This don't gotta take long, man. I need to find Dad and thought maybe you'd been seein' him, maybe you two had got up to stuff together again."

"Nope. Not since in the spring, babe. At y'all's place."

When he said "spring" Ree turned away, looked out the

window onto the gray view. Dad had let Little Arthur, Haslam Tankersly, and two Miltons, Spider and Whoop, lay low at the house for a springtime weekend. Dope of many kinds and an air of excitement came with them. Little Arthur helped Ree make sandwiches for lunch once, and seemed sort of cute going about it, then gave her a handful of mush-rooms to eat, saying they'd make fried baloney taste the way gold looks, and she ate them.

"You ain't seen him nowhere since then?"

"Huh-uh."

"He kept leavin' the house goin' someplace, though — you don't know where?"

"Got cat shit in your ears, girl?"

When the mushrooms took hold she sensed some of the gods calling to her from inside her own chest and followed their urging outside into the yard and up the sunny slope in-to the trees. She felt all gooey, gooey with the slobbered love of various gods gathered within, and smiling full-time went about the woods looking to collect butterflies and pet them until they gave milk, or maybe roll in dirt until she felt China through her skin.

"I've got to find him — he signed over all we got to go his bond. If he runs, we'll be livin' in the fields like fuckin' dogs, man."

"If I see the dude, I'll tell him that. But I ain't seen him for quite a spell now."

He'd come along behind her on the slope, and they'd bounced smiles off each other in the forest shade for a bit, then he'd hugged her to the ground and she'd felt a tremendous melting of herself, a leaking from one shape into some other form, and she'd been turned about by his hugs to kneel, and her skirt flipped up and Little Arthur knelt to join in her puddling embrace of gods and wonder.

"I got them two boys and Mom to tend, man. I need that house to help."

Little Arthur tapped a cigarette loose from a pack and struck a match.

Megan said, "Oh, good lord, baby girl — your daddy left *you* to do all that?"

"He had to, the way things go, you know."

"But all by yourself?"

Little Arthur said, "Maybe he met him a gal and went off to Memphis. He liked Memphis, I remember. That street there, all the ol'-timey boogie music'n shit. Or, *wait,* where else was it he liked? Texas! He had a real hard-on for Texas. Probly went to Texas, that's all. Or Montana — or someplace else cowboy boots look right in."

Ree never mentioned the god goo moment kneeling in the forest and he didn't, either. If not for her ripped panties she might not have later been sure it happened at all. She likely could've buried Little Arthur before the next sunset if she'd merely held those panties out to Dad and let a tear fall.

She said, "He's got other shoes, man."

"Then maybe he's wearin' 'em just about anywhere, babe — wanna snout some crank?"

"Nope."

"Blow some smoke?"

"Nope."

Little Arthur crushed his cigarette in the pie pan on the table and stood.

"Then I guess I got nothin' for you, babe. There's the door. Don't y'all bust your sweet asses goin' down that slickery hill."

Ree and Megan left together, picked their way down the steep slickery hill without sharing words. The dogs had waited on them and crashed about their legs as they stepped through snow and slid on ice, hands slapping against tree trunks for balance. At the bottom Megan grabbed Ree's shoulder, stopped her, pulled her close.

"That's sure a bad boat you been left in, ain't it?"

Ree pulled away stumbling and slipped flush to the snow. She landed with her knees splayed, skirt blown above her reddened legs, head bowed. She used both hands to raise a vast heaping of snow she mashed into her face. She blubbered her lips against the cold and rubbed her face roughly. When she lowered her hands melt and snow clung to her eyelashes, eyebrows, nostrils, lips. She said, "I'm startin' to think maybe I *do* know what the whole goddam deal is now — somebody killed Dad, and everybody knows it but me."

"Get up from there."

"He promised he'd be back with plenty for us all, but he's a promiser."

"Baby girl, I feel for you, I do, but don't do your figurin' sittin' in snow." Megan sighed, glanced at the near windows, then bent and hooked her arms under Ree's, pulled her to her feet, brushed snow from her skirt and legs. "Come on now — stand up."

"He's a goddam promiser. He'll promise anything that sets him loose."

They walked together along the unplowed road.

"Don't tell nobody it was me told you this, okay? But, the way I'm gettin' it is, you're goin' to have to go up the hill'n ask for a talk with Thump Milton."

"Thump Milton?"

"You're goin' to have to go up the hill'n hope he'll talk with you — he generally won't."

"Oh, no, no. No. That man, he scares me way more'n the rest."

"Well, scared's not a bad way to be about him, neither, hon. He's my own granpaw, been around him all my life, but I still try'n make damn sure I don't ever piss him off none. I've seen what happens. Be real careful you don't say I sent you, but he's the one who could know an answer for you. Thump's the one who could."

Megan's eyes were suddenly stuffed with water, a bulging of tears, or maybe she needed to sneeze mighty hard, sniffle. They walked on along the Hawkfall road, steps sinking into white, and Megan would not look up again until they reached her house and halted. She put an arm across Ree's shoulder, raised her other hand to point beyond the meadow of old fallen walls, up the hill to a clenched house of dun stones circled by bare trees. She said, "It's been this way with our people forever, goddam it. *For*-fuckin'-*ever*. You go see Thump. Go up there'n knock gentle on his door, and wait."

CLOUDS LOOKED to be splitting on distant peaks, dark rolling bolts torn around the mountaintops to patch the blue sky with grim. Frosty wet began to fall, not as flakes nor rain but as tiny white wads that burst as drops landing and froze a sudden glaze atop the snow. The bringing wind rattled the forest, shook limb against limb, and a wild tapping noise carried all about. Now and then a shaking limb gave up and split from the trunk to land below with a sound like a final grunt.

Ree crossed the meadow of old fallen walls, climbed uphill to Thump Milton's, but did not need to knock. A woman waited for her as she came into the yard. The woman stood on her doorstep wearing an apron over a print dress with short sleeves, rubbing her hands together, watching Ree draw near. The woman was past the middle of her years but looked pink in her cheeks, robust, with white hair brushed high into an airy poof and sprayed to stay there. She was burly, stout-boned, and flesh rolled when she moved. She said, "You've got the wrong place, I expect. Who might you be?"

Chickens were making a racket in a long low building across the yard. There was a light on inside the coop and footsteps

had crushed the snow flat between there and the back door of
the house. The house had been made without any frivolous
stones of lighthearted colors, but was entirely deep-hued and
sober. A short roof covered the woman in the doorway.

"I'm a Dolly." Ree's green hood was growing heavy from
the wet and molding to her skull while the wind chased her
skirt around her chapping legs and her eyes squinted against
the spattering weather. "My dad's Jessup Dolly. I'm Ree."

"Which Jessup would that be?"

"From Rathlin Valley. Teardrop's brother. I mean Haslam's.
Teardrop was born a Haslam."

"I believe I know who Teardrop is. That'd make your Jessup the man who married the pretty Bromont girl."

"That's right — Mom used to be Connie Bromont."

"Jack's littlest sister. I knew Jack." The woman gestured for
Ree to come up onto the steps, under the roof. She pulled
the hood away from Ree's head, looked into her face. "You
ain't here for trouble, are you? 'Cause one of my nephews is
Buster Leroy, and didn't he shoot your daddy one time?"

"Yes'm, but that ain't got nothin' to do with me. They
settled all that theirselves, I think."

"Shootin' him likely settled it. What is it you want?"

"Ma'am, I got a real bad need to talk with Thump Milton."

"Ach! Ach! Get away, girl. Away!"

"I need to, I really, really, need to, ma'am. Please — I *am a
Dolly!* Some of our blood at least is the same. That's s'posed
to *mean* somethin' — ain't that what is always said?"

The woman stalled at the mention of shared blood, sighed,

crossed her arms and pressed her lips together. She reached to touch Ree's hair, appreciated the cool dampness through her fingertips, then laid the back of her hand to Ree's winter-blushed cheek. She said, "Ain't you got no men could do this?"

"I can't wait that long."

"Well, he don't ever talk no more'n he has to, you understand that? He don't talk too direct when he does talk, neither. He says things so you ought to know what he means, but if you don't, he'll just leave it that way. And even when he does talk, he won't talk much to women."

"You could say I'm still a girl."

The woman smiled sadly, touched Ree's face again.

"I expect I won't. He'll see you for himself. You go wait in the yard somewheres by that coop and I'll tell him you're here."

There was no good sheltering spot beside the coop. A twin-trunked mimosa grew near the wall to raise a spot of windbreak and Ree crouched to the dry side of the double trunk. She crouched with her skirt dropped to ground, making a squat tent with herself as the pole. Chickens fussed inside the heated coop and melt grew an outline of ice low along the walls. The mimosa blocked direct wind, but swirls hit Ree from both sides and the bursting white wads of weather cast a mist over her that soon froze.

After most of an hour she saw a different face at the window. The woman had looked at her a few times but now the curtain eased open on a long-jawed man's face with an iron-shaded spade beard and careful fingers on the curtain. The curtain closed so subtly Ree questioned whether it had truly been open or had she wished it open and sold the wish to her eyes.

Rime of frost thickened where breath fell onto her chest.

Sleet crackled down, laid a cold sheen across everything. The afternoon sky dimmed and lights from the house carried into the yard as gleamings stretched by skidding across the ice. Tree limbs fattened with gathered silver and drooped. Dogs went home to crawl under porches.

The woman came back outside wearing a black overcoat and hat, and walked in loose harrumphing galoshes. She came into the yard but not near. She said, "He ain't likely to have time for you, child."

"I've *got* to talk to him."

"Nope. Talkin' just causes witnesses, and he don't want for any of those."

"I'll wait."

"You need to get yourself on home."

"I'll make that man weary of me out here waitin'. I've just got to talk to him."

The woman started to say something, then shook her head and returned to the house.

Ree sat chilled inside her squat tent. To occupy her mind, she decided to name all the Miltons: Thump, Blond, Catfish, Spider, Whoop, Rooster, Scrap . . . Lefty, Dog, Punch, Pink-eye, Momsy . . . Cotton, Hog-jaw, Ten Penny, Peashot . . . enough. Enough Miltons. To have but a few male names in use was a tactic held over from the olden knacker ways, the ways that had been set aside during the time of Haslam, Fruit of Belief, but returned to heartily after the great bitterness erupted and the sacred walls tumbled to nothing. Let any sheriff or similar nabob try to keep official accounts on the Dolly men when so many were named Milton, Haslam, Arthur or Jessup. The Arthurs and Jessups were the fewest, not more than five apiece, probably, and the Haslams amounted to double the Arthurs or Jessups. But the great name of the Dollys was Milton, and at least two dozen Miltons moved about in Ree's world. If you named a son Milton it was a decision that attempted to chart the life he'd live before he even stepped into it, for among Dollys the name carried expectations and history. Some names could rise to walk many paths in many directions, but Jessups, Arthurs, Haslams and Miltons were born to walk only the beaten Dolly path to the shadowed place, live and die in keeping with those blood-line customs fiercest held.

Ree and Mom both had shouted and shouted and shouted against Harold becoming a Milton, since Sonny was already a Jessup. They had shouted and won and Ree'd a thousand times wished she'd fought longer for Sonny, shouted him into an Adam or Leotis or Eugene, shouted until he was named to expect choices.

Her teeth chattered and she tried to put a tempo to the chattering, to control the shivers into a sort of chomping song. She parted her lips and snapped her teeth in step with that happy silly old song they sang in grade school about the submarine that was yellow and had everybody living in it. She snapped her teeth in time and wagged her head as though joyful even inside a shrouding of ice. The hood creaked when she moved her head, and cracked when she stood.

The woman was again in the yard. She carried a wide cup of something steaming, handed it to Ree. She said, "Soup, you crazy girl. I brung you some soup. Drink it down and be on your way."

Ree raised the cup and drank long, chewed, drank on to empty.

"Thanks."

Weather burst on the woman's hat and shoulders, wet spray jumping. She touched Ree's hood, rapped knuckles against the ice to break it fine, and swiped the pieces away.

"He knows you were in the valley, child. With Megan. And at Little Arthur's. He knows what you want to ask and he don't want to hear it."

"You mean he ain't goin' to come out'n say one word to me? Nothin'?"

The woman took the empty cup.

"If you're listenin', child, you got your answer. Now, go, get on away from here . . . and don't come back'n try'n ask him twice. Just don't."

The woman turned her back on Ree, stepped slowly toward the house. Ree watched her broad black back going away and said, "So, come the nut-cuttin', blood don't truly mean shit to him. Am I understandin' right? Blood don't truly count for diddly to *the big man*? Well, you can tell *the big man* for me I hope he has him a long, long life full of nothin' but *hiccups'n the runs*, hear? You tell him *Ree Dolly* said that."

The woman spun, glowering beneath the hat brim, and hurled the soup cup at Ree's head but missed close and the cup skipped across the glazed snow, banged into the coop. She pointed a finger and repeated, "Just don't."

SHE BECAME ice as she walked. White wads broke on her head and dripped to her shoulders to freeze and thicken. The green hood had become an ice hat and her shoulders a cold hard yoke. The scraped road had been so well iced as to be impassable, no headlights at all in the distance or near, so she walked hunched through the winter fields toward the railroad tracks. Her boots crushed the ice topping and broke into the underlying snow for traction. As long as she stomped each step she could break her way, and when she came to the sheer slope above the tracks she sat on her ass and whooshed toward the rails.

On the tracks she could walk without looking. She kept her face turned to ground, avoiding the mist from drops breaking. Her long legs flew ahead and her boots landed heavily enough. The sleet made flourish upon flourish of small popping sounds. The sleet popped small and her boots crunched through and all else was quiet.

She'd passed the meadow of old fallen walls leaving Hawk-fall, and as she considered those furiously tossed stones olden Dollys rushed to mind loud and fractious, bellowing and shaking fists. She knew few details of the old bitter reckoning that erupted inside those once holy walls, but suddenly understood to her marrow how such angers between blood could come about and last forever. Like most fights that never finished it had to've started with a lie. A big man and a lie.

The big man and prophet who'd found messages from the Fist of Gods written on the entrails of a sparkling golden fish lured with prayer from a black river way east near the sea was Haslam, Fruit of Belief. The sparkling fish had revealed signs unto him and him alone, and he'd followed the map etched tiny on the golden guts and led them all across thousands of testing miles until he hailed these lonely rugged hollows of tired rocky soil as a perfect garden spot, paradise as ordained by the map of guts sent to his eyes from the Fist of Gods.

Ree left the tracks and crossed a level field to reach the slope of caves. Weeds and grasses were made stiff by a bark of ice, shimmering and fragile, and shattered underfoot. The shimmering grasses tinkled to nothing as she kicked her feet. The caves were easy to see from below but difficult to reach. Ree snatched onto saplings to pull herself through the beating weather and up the steepness toward the slant gaping cave she knew best, the cave with a wall of stones standing in the mouth.

Haslam had been born from a god's water spit on knacker seed, shaped for manhood by a fugitive faith and sent among the Walking People to rally them and all like tinker flesh and to make a new people he'd guide to that garden place chosen by the Fist, mapped inside the sparkling fish, where they could rest their feet after six thousand years of roaming and become settled people.

The wall of stones stood across half the cave mouth and made a stout shield against the wind. Burnt remnants from many fires were strewn about the dusty cave floor. Ree bent and quickly drew together a mess of fire leavings. Log ends not consumed, charred stubs. Well back inside the cave she found a short stacking of small logs. The logs had been there a long dry while and came apart like hair clumps in her hands. Still, the logs would catch flame, and she collected the shreds.

There had been a map to this paradise, but something happened to Walking People settled with settled gods, and after but thirty years the roof of the new ways fell, walls tumbled and flew, old ways returned ravenous after the decades of slighting, and the Fist of Gods took seats in the clouds to sulk and reconsider. Ree did not know much about the religion or the ruining. The prophecies of Haslam, Fruit of Belief, reached her down the generations as hoarse godly mutterings of a big man spinning a braggish lie that made little sense and had no conclusion. The cause of the old bitter reckoning was not clear, either, and there might've been living Dollys who knew the truth but nobody ever said it where she could hear. All they ever said was there'd been a woman.

Ree shed her coat, the hooded sweatshirt, the wet skirt. They landed heavily, lumps of fabric clotted with ice. She had a fair pile of punk wood laid in the corner by the stone wall but no kindling, and once in from the weather she was loath to go back into it. *It was those brute ancient ways that broke fresh over her world at every dawn and sent Dollys to let the blood drain from Dad's heart and dump his flesh somewhere hidden from path and cloud.* Her boots felt stiff as iron but she kept them on. She slid her panties down, stepped out of them, then raised her undershirt overhead and off. Bare skin but for boots she crouched to the woodpile and stuck the dry garments beneath the likeliest charred stubs and hairy clumps. She had one book of matches and half a doobie in the coat. She held her breath while striking a match, carefully touched the flame to an edge of her panties and mercifully they browned fast, then puffed into flame.

The fire seemed to have been waiting to be born for it scooted quickly from flickers to a roaring flame. The flames pulsed and brightened the cave mouth. The light met Ree and glowed on her skin and cast her shadow up. She stamped her feet and stared out from the cave onto a forest vista sunk beneath ice. Some trees sagged near to snapping, some snapped.

She peed near the entrance to let animals know she was visiting.

After the bitter reckoning many Dollys fled from Hawkfall to caves, and this slope was where they congregated to live through that first winter of exile. Her Dollys were among those Dollys. Her people had lived hunkered in these caves for a mean winter and late spring, kids breathing rattly, grannies spoiling in the dank, the men with each breath refreshing that great snarling tribal anger that Haslam had tried to preach away from their hearts and habits.

She mended the fire when it faltered with clumps and stubs and grew the flames higher than her knees. As she warmed she moved, shuffle-stepped with arms raised and tossed her hands to jab, jab, hook, overhand right, broad shadows punching against the cave wall. *Flick them left jabs to open 'em up, girl, then bang the right to put 'em down.*

The cave was long and had two more rooms, at least, deeper down and chill, but the space behind the wall warmed quickly. Ree shook her clothes, batted the ice away, and spread them near the fire. She lit the half doobie. Hunters and lovers had used the cave in recent years and had left their withered litter and bent empties, but there was some ancestral trash made visible by the lifting flames. Parts of several fragile white plates and cup handles, a tarnished long fork with two tines, cracked blue potion bottles and tin cans thinned by time to where a finger could poke through.

They likely buried him somewhere near.

If they buried him.

Or dropped him into a bottomless black hole.

The sleet stopped after night fell. The sky spread low and milky over all that ice. Time and again Ree slipped into Mamaw's coat and hunted wood on the slope. The milk sky and ice let her see dead wood and she dragged the wood to the fire, made the flames healthy, and hung the coat to dry. The corner by the wall became very warm and Ree sat there bare-butted and oddly comforted, knowing that so many relatives with names she never knew had hunched here in this very spot to renew themselves after a sad spinning time had dropped over their lives and whirled them raw.

Coyotes sang to her and she slept, fed the fire, heard snowplows way in the distance.

Her belly rumbled and pinged and hunger drew her into an aching curl.

Water woke her. The blessing of daylight showed a warmer world and thin rivulets trickled down the slope. The air at dawn was warmer than any day had been for a week. The landscape was softening some but not to mush. A freight passed on the tracks beyond the field and whisked the path clear.

He'd fight if he knew they were comin' and maybe somebody else's hurt, too.

She stood in sunlight and stretched, a great long body pale and twisting at the brink of a cave. She walked to water dripping from the rock above the cave mouth, cupped her hands to the trickle and drank and drank deeply of the falling new water.

HILLSIDES KNIT with ice came apart. Ice slipped from everything, limb, twig, stump, rock, and cascaded chinking to ground. Mist lifted from the bottoms to lie over the tracks but did not lift much above her head. Mist smeared like tears squashed on her cheeks. She could see the sky but her feet were cloudy. The stout ties, moistened, released their tar smell, and she kicked from one wet tie to the next, sniffing tar in the mist and listening to ice chime in the trees or slip loose to shatter. She wiped the mist that felt like tears on her cheeks and pulled her hood tight. Larger ice shapes fell thudding. Runnels of high melt cut wee downhill gutters in the snow. Ice sounds and trickle sounds and her boots thumping. At a bridge across a frozen creek she paused to stare down. She tried to see past the pocked skin of ice to the depths of flowing water. She was strangely still and staring, still and staring on the bridge until she understood that her eyes searched for a body beneath that ice, and she crouched to her knees and cried, cried until tears ran down her chest.

IN THE house she slept, and when she woke the sun was red falling west and everybody wanted food. She splashed her face at the kitchen sink, dried on a crusted towel. A pot full of odd-looking food she could not name sat on the stove, a creation of the boys from the supper before. It smelled like soup but looked like bloodied mashed potatoes. Mom was in her rocker clutching a wooden spoon and the boys sat wrapped in quilts watching television, a public TV gardening show offering tips on how best to grow row upon row of spiffy plants you never got to eat.

"Hey," she said, "what is it in this pot on the stove?"

Harold came to her, quilt over his head, face peeking out. He looked into the pot, sniffed, puckered and frowned.

"That was supper," he said. "Me'n Sonny made it when you never came home. Mom reckoned we cooked it too much."

"What is it?"

"Basketti."

"That's what that is? How'd you make it?"

"Tomato soup and noodles."

"Looks awful gluey. You boil them noodles separate, or in the soup?"

"In the soup. Why mess two pots?"

"That ain't how you make basketti. You boil the noodles separate."

"But that way you got two pots to wash."

Ree pinched his cheek, opened the cupboard, shoved the few cans around, then said, "I don't think I can save that glop with nothin' we got. Toss it behind the shed."

Ree set the big black skillet on the stove and sparked a flame. She pulled the bacon grease can from the bottom shelf of the fridge and scooped a cup or two into the skillet. She cleaned potatoes and onions, chopped them, and dropped them hissing into the fat. She salted and peppered and the smell ranged to the front room, called Sonny to the kitchen.

Sonny said, "I could eat that much myself."

"Take this and flip 'em when —"

Quick steps on the porch and the door flew open and Blond Milton stood there pointing at her. He said, "You know, there's people goin' 'round sayin' you best *shut up.*" Blond Milton was a grandfather in age but not in manner, square-shouldered and flat-bellied, fair-haired with ruddy skin, and generally wore fancy cowboy shirts over starched jeans ironed into a stiff crease. He was most always shaved clean, barbered, talced, smelling of bay rum and armed with two pistols. "People you oughta listen to, too." He held the door open and waved for her to follow him outside. She grabbed her coat and met him on the porch and he flung her down the steps onto the scree of ice that had fallen from the eaves during the day. "Get up'n get your ass in the truck. Get your ass in there."

Harold and Sonny stood in the doorway watching as she pulled herself to her feet. Harold had his mouth open and Sonny had his eyes narrowed. He stepped forward and said, "You don't get to hit my sister."

"Druther I hit you, Sonny? 'Cause I will if you want."

"Boys! Go back in, boys. Cook those taters 'til they brown. Cook 'em brown, Harold, then be sure to turn the fire off. Go on."

Sonny came down two steps, said, "Nobody gets to hit my sister who ain't her brother."

Blond Milton fairly beamed looking at his seed Sonny standing there defiant with fists balled and jaw set. He smiled a twisty proud smile, then stepped over and swatted Sonny flush in the face with an open hand. The swat knocked Sonny to his rump. Blond Milton said, "Balls is good, Sonny, but don't let 'em make you into a idiot."

Bubbles of blood puffed from Sonny's nostrils and burst to speck his lips.

Ree said, "Dad'd kill you for that."

"*Shit*, I whipped your daddy about twice a year since *he* was a kid."

"You *never* whipped him as *a man* in your *life!* Not when he wasn't too fucked up to punch."

Blond Milton grabbed her by the coat sleeve, pulled her toward his truck.

"Get your dumb ass in there. I got someplace to show you."

He drove fast on the rut road, turned west on the blacktop.

His bay rum smell filled the cab and Ree cracked a window. The truck was a big white Chevy with a red camper shell. There was a mattress in the shell. Blond Milton drove a truck with a mattress in the camper shell but he never went camping and his wife hated the very idea of the truck but never said so to him. He ran a crew of pot farmers and crank cooks that often included Jessup, always had cash, and folks said he was the Dolly who'd years before stepped forward and shot the two Gypsy Jokers who'd come south from Kansas City figuring their loud scary biker reputations would let them muscle in on the yokels and take control.

"Where're we goin'?"

"Down the road."

"Down the road to where?"

"To somewhere you need to see."

They drove past deep woodlands and ranges of snow. The sun was behind the hills, the last western light made a sky of four blues, and the gaunt trees on the high ridges were stark in relief. Crows sat on limbs and looked like black buttons on twilight.

Just beyond the one-lane bridge across Egypt Creek, Blond Milton gunned the truck up a washboard rise and along a crooked lane. He drove until he reached the drive to a house in the near distance, then parked. The house had burned. Three walls and part of the roof still stood, but the walls were blackened and the roof was blown open in the center with sections slanted away in every direction.

Ree said, "What're you parkin' here for? Man, I ain't gettin' back there in that camper!"

"You think I'm wantin' to fuck *you*?"

"If you are, you'll be fuckin' me dead! That's the only way."

"Jesus, but you're sure 'nough twelve to the dozen, know it? Just quit kickin' a minute and listen." Blond Milton turned to face her. "Why I parked here is to show you that house." Dark was near full but the snowscape had caught and held light, so the house remained visible. "That right there's the last place me or anybody seen Jessup. The other fellas went off doin' things'n when they got back that's what they got back to, only it still had fire goin'."

Ree looked at the ruined house, the splintered roof, charred wood, walls licked black by flame.

"He never blew no lab before."

"I know it. But somethin' musta jumped wrong this time."

"He's known for *never* fuckin' up labs nor cookin' bad batches. He's known for knowin' what he's doin'."

"You cook long enough, this's bound to happen."

Ree opened the door, lowered one foot, said, "You sayin' Dad's in there burnt to a crisp?"

"I'm sayin' that's the last place me or anybody else seen him. That's what I'm tellin' you."

She stepped out, eyes on the house, boots in snow.

"I'm goin' up for a look."

"Whoa, whoa, whoa! No, you ain't! Get back in here. That shit's all *poison*, girl. *Toxic*. It'll eat the skin clean off your bones and wilt the bones, too. It'll turn your lungs to paper sacks and *tear holes* in 'em. Don't you get nowheres near that fuckin' house."

"If Dad's in there dead, I'm collectin' him and carryin' him home to bury."

"Stay the hell away from that house!"

The snow on the drive to the house was unmarked by boot or hoof or claw. Ree hustled up the slight rise, glancing backwards at Blond Milton. He did not give chase and she slowed. She kept at a distance from the walls, began circling in the pure snow. One wall had flown into the yard. Windows had exploded and the frames dangled, blackened with glass fingers clinging. The charred wood smelled. There were other acrid smells. She circled through snowdrifts to the back. There was a trash pile topped with a cap of snow. Big brown glass jugs, cracked funnels, white plastic bottles, garden hose. She edged slowly between the trash pile and the house. She could see well enough. The kitchen sink had snagged on floorboards falling through to dirt and the curved faucet poked up amidst the blackened wood. Horseweed turned white stood chin-high in the floorboard holes. There were humps of ash where furniture had been. A round wall clock had cooked black and fallen in the heat to become puddled across the stovetop. The stove was wedged partway down a hole in the floor and . . . horseweed. Horseweed turned white stood chin-high in the floorboard holes.

Ree eased back from the house, whirled on her heels, and walked briskly to Blond Milton.

"We can get."

"You did right to not go in there."

"You showed me the place'n we can get now."

"It's always a bad deal when these things blow. Jessup'n me maybe had our tussles, but he was my first cousin still. I'll see whatever I can do for you."

She did not speak all the way home. She gouged herself to keep from speaking. She counted barns to keep from speaking, counted fence posts, counted vehicles that were not pickup trucks. She bit her lips and clamped with her teeth, counting for distraction while faintly tasting blood.

Blond Milton took the rut road that led to his side of the creek. He parked near the three houses. They got out and stood beside the truck. He said, "I know losin' Jessup leaves you-all hurtin' over there. I know it's a lot to handle. Too much, probably."

"We'll make do."

"Me'n Sonya talked about it'n we feel we could take Sonny off your hands. Not Harold, I don't reckon, but we'd take Sonny. We could help you that much."

"You *what?*"

"We could take Sonny for you and raise him up the rest of the way."

"My ass, you will."

"Watch your mouth with me, girl. We'd raise the boy way better'n you'n that momma of yours can, that's for certain sure. Maybe on down the line we'd take Harold, too."

Ree started walking fiercely toward the narrow footbridge. He snatched at her arm from behind but she spun away. On the flat bridge she paused and called, "You son of a bitch. You go straight to hell'n fry in your own lard. Sonny'n Harold'll die livin' in a fuckin' cave *with me'n Mom* before they'll ever spend a single fuckin' night with *you*. Goddam you, Blond Milton, you must think I'm a stupid idiot or somethin' — there's horseweed standin' *chin-high* inside that place!"

REE SLAMMED the door behind herself and stomped past the boys, clomping loudly to the closet in her own room. She reached behind the rank of skirts and dresses hanging, into the far hidden corner, and retrieved two long guns. She dropped boxes of shells into a pocket of Mamaw's coat. She cradled the guns in her arms, jerked her head at the watching boys, and led them to the side porch. She turned on the porch light and rested the weapons upright against the rail, then began to load them.

"I wasn't sure just when you boys'd need to know about shootin', but I think maybe now it's time you do. Now's when you boys start learnin' how to shoot guns at what *needs* shootin'. Throw some cans'n stuff out on that slope there. Set 'em up standin' so they'll keel over when you hit 'em."

Sonny and Harold bounced to it with glee. They rooted eagerly in the trash heap and started arranging targets on the slope of snow. The bright porch light laid long menacing shadows behind the targets.

She said, "No bottles. The glass'll wash down to the yard

in spring'n I'll be doctorin' your feet all goddam summer. Just cans or plastic, stuff like that."

One gun was a double-barreled 20 gauge, a strikingly handsome heirloom shotgun with a creamy blond stock. The other was an old and abused .22 rifle with a busted stock put back together by brass screws, a semi-automatic that held sixteen shorts. Ree'd learned to shoot on these very weapons, trained in the fields by Dad, and had a deep fondness for them because of that. The shotgun was the prettiest thing she owned and she'd used it to take rabbits, dove, and quail. The .22 was for harvesting squirrels from trees or frogs from ponds and plunking armadillos rooting holes in the yard.

She held the shotgun, said, "This trigger shoots this barrel, this one shoots this one. There's hardly goin' to be any time ever when you need both barrels at once, but if what you got to shoot is somethin' *big'n mean,* pull 'em both and splatter the fuckin' thing. For these cans'n stuff, though, just shoot one barrel at a time."

She started them both on the shotgun. She steadied their arms and guided their fingers on the trigger. Snow jumped where they shot and each blast rocked the shooter backwards.

"You think you can't miss with a shotgun, but you can. You still gotta aim good."

Harold said, "Holy cow, that's loud!"

"Uh-huh, it is kind of, ain't it?"

The boys shot hell out of the snowy slope. They exploded cans, milk cartons, boxes, and each explosion tossed snow and dirt briefly aloft and scattered. They shot *boom-boom, plink-plink-plink,* and the scent of shooting spread on the wind. Ree made suggestions, patted heads, loaded weapons.

She counted shells and kept the boys shooting until but a handful for each gun remained.

"That's it," she said. She spread her arms in the night and nodded while inhaling the smell of shooting. "We've raised enough ruckus for now."

Sonny walked to the slope and began to boot the blasted targets. He stomped shot cans flat and kicked shot boxes into the dark, doing a short hop from one victim to the next, humming as his pounding feet finished the wounded.

"Man, that shootin' is major fun!" Harold said.

"It can be."

"When do we get to do it more?"

"I'll try'n get shells at Bawbee pretty soon."

Sonny paused in the middle of a stomp, looked toward the side of the house and suddenly moved that way.

"Hey, who's that comin'?"

Ree stepped from the porch with the shotgun at her side and Harold followed, toting the rifle. The crunch of oncoming footsteps carried. A bent-over shape was slowly edging around the house into the side yard, hoisting something bulky.

The shape saw Ree and the boys and the weapons, halted, tried to raise its arms but could not raise the bulky thing overhead, and said, "Goddam, Sweet Pea! It's just me'n my baby! What in blue blazes is everybody doin' with a gun out over here?"

On hearing that voice Ree broke her tense stride and ran joyously to Gail's side. She held the shotgun swaying low and leaned to kiss the crown of Gail's head. She snorted, laughed, gave a joshing shove, and said, "I *knew* you wouldn't eat shit *long.* I know you good enough to know *that.* I knew you'd get back to yourself'n show up for me. I just *knew.*"

Gail touched her free hand to the shotgun and raised the barrel until it pointed at the sky. She said, "What on earth gives?"

A PICNIC OF words fell from Gail's mouth to be gathered around and savored slowly. Ree's feelings could stray from now and drift to so many special spots of time in her senses when listening to that voice, the perfect slight lisp, the wet tone, that soothing hillfolk drawl. She nodded and nodded, drifting while absently forking fried potatoes straight from the black skillet. She paused with the fork stalled midway between her mouth and the frying pan.

Gail went on, "He told me he wanted to go check his deer stand — you believe that baloney? In all this snow'n icy mess he decides along toward dark he's just gotta drive out to Lilly Ridge right now'n look at his stinkin' ol' deer stand. *Again*." Gail sat on a kitchen chair and Ned lay on the table, restful inside a plastic baby carrier that had a thin swinging handle. A big soft blue bag with a shoulder strap sat on the floor, full of baby stuff. "I know when he says *deer stand* it means he's gone over to fuck Heather. Where else could he be goin'? Ain't nobody needs to check on their deer stand *twice* a week. At *night*. Sayin' *deer stand* just means . . . It's her who was his girl-friend forever. It's her who he really loves. It's her who he wants. I'm just what he's got."

The fork reached Ree's mouth and she swallowed while sighing. She squirted more ketchup on the brown leavings stuck to the skillet bottom, scraped. She said, "I think he got awful lucky to get you, Sweet Pea. I always have thought that."

"He loves Heather. Me'n Ned's just the booby prizes he's stuck with instead of what he wanted." Gail raised her head, shrugged, then snickered. "But Floyd's not all that mean, really, he's just a liar who don't bother to come up with lies you can swallow."

"Those kinds of liars are the worst. They're lyin' to you'n callin' you stupid in the same breath, with the same words."

"I know, I know, but piss on him and his stinkin' deer stand, anyhow — how goes it with your troubles?"

Ree licked her fork shiny and dropped it into the skillet, wiped her lips with two fingers. She flapped a hand toward the boys, shook her head, said, "I don't want to say while we're sittin' here."

"Still need to get down to Reid's Gap?"

"Yup. That might be the one last place worth checkin'."

Gail raised a key ring and jingled it while grinning. She said, "Got the in-laws' old truck."

Ree brightened and smiled and said, "You are who I always did think you were, Sweet Pea. You truly are." She bent over and began to unlace her boots. "Let me get dry socks on'n we'll head out."

The boys watched television, some masterpiece show about dandies with fancy stagecoaches and houses like castles and different accents. Mom sat in her rocker staring at the baby with alarm, pondering wretchedly, tired face riffling between shimmers of suspicion and guilt, as though trying hard to recollect if maybe she could've birthed yet another little bundle who'd somehow already slipped from memory. Gail snacked on animal crackers from a small box in the blue bag. She studied Mom's face as she chewed. She reached to pat Mom on the arm, get her attention.

"This baby's my baby boy, Ned."

"Is he? I have so many days I can't picture."

"Uh-huh, he is. You know it's been quite a while since I seen you, Mom. How *are* you? How're *you* doin'?"

"The same."

"Still just the same?"

"Different kinds of same."

"Well, your hair looks nice."

Ree stood and tapped her boots against the stove, getting the fit right. She said, "Mom. Mom, we've got to run down to Reid's Gap for a little bit. See somebody."

Mom's expression settled and she turned her head away from the baby, toward the television. Hounds in a huge pack were gathered on a damp brick street outside an ancient chapel being blessed for the hunt by a wan but wordy reverend while men in red coats sat lordly atop beautiful jostling horses waiting for the amen. She said, "Have fun."

The night cold made flimsy ice on the steps. Gail carried Ned swinging and Ree held her by the arm going down to the truck. The truck was antique in age, with a long wobbly gearshift to the floor and a bench seat. The sitting spots were worn open to the hairy stuffing and poking wires. Gail laid Ned in the middle and Ree sat beside him. The engine kicked alive with a loud chuff and black puffs from the tailpipe scudded low across the snowy yard.

The moon was a blue dot glowing behind moody clouds.

Gail said, "Does Mom know what's goin' on?"

"I don't think so."

"Don't you think you should tell her?"

"Huh-uh."

"Why not?"

"It'd be too mean to tell her. This is just exactly the sort of shit she went crazy to get away from."

"I guess she couldn't help any, anyhow."

"Nope. It's on me."

The truck bounced high along the rut road and tilted this way and that. The snow had been compacted by warmer hours and lay thin, but there were pits in the rock and dirt the truck had to be gentled over to avoid scraping bottom. There were scads of shallower potholes and spring floodwaters had cut creases in the dirt hubcap-deep. Ree held Ned's carrier steady with her left hand. Gail said, "You-all's road has got rough to where you about can't call it a road no more."

"You've been sayin' that since third grade."

"Well, it was true in the third grade and it's done nothin' but get truer since then."

"We like it this way — it keeps tourists out."

"That's the same ol' joke your dad told me the first time I ever rode in here."

"I think he meant it, though."

"I think he *must've,*" Gail said. She squeaked the truck to a stop at the blacktop. "Which way is this place?"

"Go towards Dorta, then take that road there that heads south past Strawn Bottoms. You know the one, right? Then it's just a little ways further across the line."

"Oh. Now I'm thinkin' maybe I *have* been there before. Is this the place where they got all the blueberries? The ones you pick yourself?"

"Yup. They got acres and acres of them berries. I never did do any pickin' when I was down there, though."

Ned gurgled and goo-gooed, opened his eyes slow as a school day and closed them at the same pace. He wore a little skullcap that tied under his chin and was wrapped fat with a sky blue blanket. The truck smelled of baby powder and drooled milk crusty on the blanket and stale butts in the ashtray. When headlights passed going the other way and Gail squinted against the light, her hand instinctively reached to protect the baby.

Gail said, "My daddy fell by yesterday, brought me some more of my clothes'n stuff, and I asked him if he knew where your dad might be. He wouldn't really look at me when I asked, so I asked again, and all he said was, 'Go nurse your boy.'"

"I know, Sweet Pea."

"It gave me a flat bad feelin' when he answered like that."

"He's probly right."

Ree sat with one hand on the baby and her eyes on Gail. Passing cars lit her behind the wheel in quick stuttering glimpses, her wry curled lips, freckled bony cheeks, and those hurt brown eyes. She watched Gail's hand move from steering wheel to gearshift as the road rolled up and down and around the dark country. She watched her hand reach toward Ned and touch his baby nose as they crossed the Twin Forks River on a skeletal iron bridge and could hear the cold water humming south.

Gail said, "This road here, ain't it?"

"Yup."

The first time Ree kissed a man it was not a man, but Gail acting as a man, and as the kissing progressed and Gail acting as a man pushed her backwards onto a blanket of pine needles in shade and slipped her tongue deep into Ree's mouth, Ree found herself sucking on the wiggling tongue of a man in her mind, sucking that plunging tongue of the man in her mind until she tasted morning coffee and cigars and spit leaked from between her lips and down her chin. She opened her eyes then and smiled, and Gail yet acting the man roughed up her breasts with grabs and pinches, kissed her neck, murmuring, and Ree said, *"Just like that! I want it to be just like that!"* There came three seasons of giggling and practice, puckering readily anytime they were alone, each being the man and the woman, each on top and bottom, pushing for it with grunts or receiving it with sighs. The first time Ree kissed a boy who was not a girl his lips were soft and timid on hers, dry and unmoving, until finally she had to say it and did, *"Tongue, honey, tongue,"* and the boy she called honey turned away saying, *"Yuck!"*

There were five streets and two stop signs in Reid's Gap. Snow was piled high in the parking lot of the elementary school and the Get'n Quik store was the only building with lights on. A field of crashed vehicles butted against the road through town, and these trophies for bad luck from many eras spread crumpled downhill beyond sight. Yard sale signs on sticks were stuck in the ground at corners. Flyers for Slim Ted's Tuesday Square Dances at Ash Flat were tacked to telephone poles. Churches stood at both ends of town and a windowless senior center at the heart.

Ree said, "Her house is yellow, just off this road, here. It ain't far, I don't think. It's a sort of pretty little place. Wait — turn in here."

"I thought you said yellow."

"She must've painted."

April Dunahew had a rail fence across the face of her yard and bordering the driveway. A rose arbor stood over the sidewalk shoveled clean and the house lights were bright. The house was now an ordinary white with green shutters. Gnarled evergreen shrubs grew squatty along the walls. A small car and a long truck that had a business name written on the side were parked in the drive. The door had a bell that made music of four ringing tones.

The porch light came on and the door eased back. April wore a black dress that draped waistless to her ankles and eyeglasses hooked to a glinting chain. She had blond hair curled springy and a ready smile. She said, "Is that . . . ?"

"Ree. It's me."

"You've cut your hair!"

"I got tired of it hangin' to my butt'n bein' in my way all the time."

"I *loved* that wild-ass hair of yours. Just loved it."

"You never had to rake the leaves out of it every night like me. Plus it's grown back pretty good since spring, anyhow.

April, this girl is my friend Gail Lockrum, and that's her boy, Ned."

"You keep forgettin' it's Gail *Langan* now."

"Oops, slipped my mind again — she got married. To a Langan."

April said, "Married's a good thing to be once you've got yourself a baby. That's how I still think. That's my two cents, anyhow. Why'n't you-all come on in and we'll sit."

"I'm here huntin' Dad."

"I was guessin' that."

The house was by far the most pleasant Ree had ever been allowed to enter. Everything was where it was supposed to be and clean. The furniture had been costly and there were elegant built-in bookcases flanking the fireplace and a dozen special little touches. A carved wooden hutch stood against the wall, featuring an arrangement of delicate blown-glass objects of many odd colors and complicated shapes. A staircase that curved led upstairs and the wooden steps shined all the way up. A television was on in the family room and a man's head was visible above the line of the couch. April pulled slatted double doors closed to mute the television noise.

"Now, you know me'n Jessup quit keepin' company a good while ago."

"I figured, but thought maybe you'd still know a thing or two."

"Well, I'm kind of afraid I might. I've been wonderin'." April reached under the couch and pulled out a metal cookie tray that held a small pile of pot and a pipe. "I'm goin' to need to kick myself back for this, Ree. Bear with me."

It had seemed like a mumbled sunny song to stay here
nursing April back when. April had notions in her head that
were loosed in her days. April kept puking and voiding wet
gushes in the mornings until one day she rose tottering to
treat the sick spirits of this house with burning sage, make the
house well to make herself well. She carried a blue smudge
pot full of sand and a sheaf of smoking sage and aimed the
smoke into corners and doorways, her eyes closed and her lips
silently saying stuff that added churchy oomph to the powers
of the smoke. She smoked away haints so the house could feel
cleansed of lingering angers and pains and bad ideas that
clung to old shadows soaked into the walls. She waved smoke
to make the house well so she could get well, and while the
house freshly stank of sage the wellness spread from the walls
to her tummy, and the next morning she did not puke or void
wet gushes. By noon she was sipping vodka from a coffee cup.

"You still bad on the bottle?"

"No. No. I give that up. It's just beer nowadays, and some
of this."

The pipe crossed the room a few times while the man
watching television snored and Ned slept. Smoke curled
toward the ceiling and spread into a calm flat layer below the
light. April said, "Right around when he was arrested this last
time, me'n Jessup had a little rekindle happen. I'd started
seein' Hubert in there months before. He's a good man'n
we're meant for each other and all, I guess, but your dad
always did tickle me extra, don't you know. Jessup'n me run
across each other by total accident out at the trout place by
Rockbridge, and he got me to laughin' so happy things

rekindled for a day or two, then he was gone again. Saw hide nor hair for a spell, but about, maybe, three or four weeks back, I had stopped at Cruikshank's Tap on the state line, and he was in there drinkin'. He was with three fellas who looked a little rougher even than Jessup usually looked. They didn't look to be havin' no fun, either, nor wantin' to."

"Was one of them three a crusty little bastard?"

"They all were pretty crusty-lookin'."

"Dad say anything?"

"That's what has made me feel so hinky'n blue since — he looked square at me but acted like he didn't know me, never seen me before. They were leavin' in a knot and I stood in the way at the door, but he went brushin' past me without even a nod. Somethin' ugly was up with them fellas. Somethin' real wrong was goin' on, and since then I've gone over it and over it in my head and think I finally get why he didn't even nod my way. He was protectin' me, see, by ignorin' me. That's when I understood your dad had loved me. I understood it from how he'd looked away."

ROCKS HELD long by the hillside slipped loose in the melt and scattered downhill to flatten one corner of a hog-pen fence, and fifty hogs roused in the night and shoved through the sudden gap onto the road. The hogs were big and curious and rooted over to the bridge and stood there, blocking traffic. The Twin Forks River rushed along cold and black but streaked yellow, danced upon brightly by headlights. Three or four vehicles had been forced to stop on either side of the bridge. A farmer and his wife with flashlights and sticks and one dog were trying to turn the hogs around and herd them back through the gap in the fence.

Gail said, "Remember when we were little? When Catfish Milton kept hogs, and they told us to go feed 'em corn once, but we didn't understand how hogs with no hands could *ever* manage to eat corn straight from the cob, so you'n me hunkered our dumb asses down'n rubbed the kernels off of *all them cobs?* Remember that?"

"Yup."

"We *thought* we were showin' good sense. My fingers hurt a month, it seemed like."

"They laughed at us a long time for that day."

The truck was first in line on the south side of the bridge. The hogs were big grunting humps milling about the bridge and road shoulder. A couple of drivers had gotten out to help the farmer and his wife, but the hogs smelled something fresh in the night and were not easily turned around. Ned began to cry and Gail said, "Him needs some suck, don't him? Him's hungry for milk and Momma's late givin' him his nipple."

"You goin' to nurse him right here?"

"Why not? I don't seem to make milk like I should oughta, but what milk I make him gets, and him's hungry now."

Gail unbuttoned her blouse and pulled the front wide. She undid her bra and let it dangle to her belly. She raised Ned from the basket and his little pink mouth clamped onto a nipple. Ree leaned forward to look closely at the baby's lips sucking and the heavy bare breasts, and said, "Man, them peaches got big!"

"They ain't goin' to stay that way."

"I feel like a fuckin' carpenter's dream, lookin' at them things!"

"They'll poof down again before too long."

"You should get you a picture while they last."

"I guess I probly should. They can flatten out pretty bad once they poof back down."

Ree watched Gail hold Ned as closely as anyone could ever be held, feed him supper from a part of her own body, and saw in them a living picture illustrating one kind of future. The looming expected kind of future and not one she wanted. Ned's baby mouth sucked and sucked on that nipple like he was fixing to drain Gail to the dregs. She said, "I reckon I'll go'n help kick them hogs off the road. We'll be settin' here all night, the way it's goin'."

"Don't let 'em eat you."

"I doubt I taste all that sweet."

The hogs were boiling about the bridge, grunting to the far end, then being chased back with sticks. They shrieked when whacked and raced briefly in any direction, slamming one another, slamming the rails, knocking various people to ground. Ree edged across the bridge and began to shoo the hogs, *sooey, sooey!* toward the gap in the fence. So many headlights shining from both sides of the bridge made it difficult to see clearly. Squealing hump shadows rushed about between the beams. Ree stood near the black rail and when she felt humps bumping her legs or passing near she gave them the boot and more loud shooing. Once the bridge had been cleared a couple of leader hogs finally waddled down from the road and through the gap and others followed.

The farmer watched the hogs going back into the pen, swabbed sweat from his face with a sleeve, sighed, then said, "For cripes sake! There's two run out on the bridge again."

Ree said, "I'll get up there behind 'em and aim 'em this way for you."

"It'd sure be a help if you could, missy."

The fleeing hogs were halted by the small circle of folks standing at the north end of the bridge. Their hooves skidded on the road surface. They came to a complete stop and stood there looking into the many blinding headlight beams. The people were smoking and laughing, joking about the great

bounty of free hams and sides of bacon that had been running around available in the night without anybody grabbing
so much as a hock to haul home. The hogs moved slowly to
the bridge rail and walked toward a spot where no people
stood. Ree saw their plan and loped ahead of them, turned
about and kicked limply at their snouts. "Sooey! Sooey that-
away!"

It was the sound of the motor that caused her to look over
her shoulder. She'd spent so many long days and longer nights
of her life listening for that motor, had so many bursts of
relief upon finally hearing that certain memorized rattle and
squeak of Dad's Capri coming down the rut road to the
house, that her body and spirit responded automatically to
the sound. Wings beat in her tummy and her eyes squinted
searching into the various lights. There were now seven or
eight vehicles on the north side and she wended through the
thicket of beams, hands held to shade her eyes, toward the
imprinted rattle and squeak of the family car. She waved her
arms overhead, gesturing into the maze of headlights. The
hogs followed her off the bridge and she paid them no mind,
but began to move quickly along the line of vehicles, waving
her hands all the while. She positioned herself to be easily
recognized, stood tall facing north, and saw the Capri at the
rear of the line as it backed up, turned about in a hurry, and
sped away uphill along the road toward Bawbee.

Ree stared briefly after the twin red taillights as they
climbed the hill, the red easily visible against the night and
general white of the landscape. She breathed hesitant shallow
breaths watching the red dots climb, then raced back across

the bridge, combat boots drumming hard on the old iron, and yanked the truck door. Gail was bent over the bench seat fussing with a diaper from the blue bag while she tried to change Ned. She had yet to button her blouse or clean his behind and he lay in yellow poop while her breasts swayed above his face. She looked up when the door flew open so violently, and said, "What?"

"Dad! Dad's Capri was over across the bridge! He took off toward Bawbee — see them taillights?"

"You *sure* it was him?"

"It's *our* car."

"Ree, we're still sort of a little bit stoned — you *sure* you saw him?"

"I ain't so stoned I don't know our own goddam car when I see it! And that's what I just fuckin' saw — *let's get after him.*"

Gail leaned over and began to tuck herself away, button her blouse.

"Well, you've got to finish changin' Ned's diaper, then. You do that'n I'll chase. Or else you'll have to wait a minute while I do."

Ree sniffed the scent of baby shit in the air, looked at the yellow smear, the helpless drooling face, then reached beneath Ned and pulled him and his fouled diaper onto her lap.

"I got him."

Gail put the truck into gear and lunged forward across the bridge. She drove slowly past the line of waiting vehicles with the people standing about and two hogs yet running around, then stomped the gas pedal flat and chased her own headlights up the thin winding road. She got the speed up to where the high-set old truck felt loose and tilty on the turns. If you lost the road there was no shoulder and it was a smashing drop into lonesome wooded gullies. She kept her foot heavy on the gas and crossed into the far lane on tough curves.

She said, "I've lost them taillights."

"Get around this bend'n maybe we'll see him ahead down in the bottoms." Ree was trying to wipe Ned's butt with a blank section of the dirty diaper while jolting about in darkness inside a speeding truck that leaned toward tilt on the curves. She aimed her swiping fingers at the baby soil but her hands bounced about and she felt her knuckles sink in muck and slide across smooth skin. She wiped her fingers on the diaper, raised Ned a bit, and swabbed his baby butt until it looked close enough to clean in the shadows. "I don't see taillights nowhere now."

The truck said warning stuff on the turns in a grating metal language. The tall shifter shook about angrily and the black knob ducked away from Gail's hand until she let up on the gas pedal. "Man, I can't go this fast!" The truck coughed and heaved as it lost speed. "That's too fast for this ol' thing to go safe." The road was black to the eye and always turning, one long dark loop dropping sharply toward the bottoms. The truck passed between glum forests of plucked trees and clots of shivering pine. "It won't do no good for nobody if we slide off this goddam ridge."

"Ugh — where's a clean one?"

"Clean one what?"

"Diaper."

"It fell to the floor, there, by your feet."

"I don't trust myself to stick in pins rollin' around like this."

"He sprung for some store-bought kind. They don't call for pins."

Black ice lay slick where the road bottomed, and the truck slid a surprise twist sideways and completed most of a circle before rubber found dry asphalt again and Gail yanked the squealing tires straight. She yelped and slowed fearfully to a shambling pace, then suddenly stopped altogether and sat trembling, overlooking a steep bank of scrub and a frozen cow pond. Her pale hands remained choked around the steering wheel. Beyond the pond there were shorn open acres of stumps and snow and deep drifts built against stacks of felled trees. She bowed her head to the wheel. She said, "Sweet Pea, this ain't what we got stoned to do."

During the brief spin Ree had clutched Ned bare-assed and squirming to her chest. She'd held him fast with both hands while whirled about to slam her shoulder against the door and smack her cheek against the window glass. Now she cradled his head to her chest with one hand and spread the diaper on her lap with the other and felt an odd blush rise on her face. She started to laugh with relief and said, "Well, you never do know for sure *what* you're gettin' stoned to do. That's a big part of why you do it." She calmly began to wrap and fold the diaper snug around Ned's voiding spouts and he smiled a winning toothless smile. "I think he looks a way lot more like you than him, know it?"

"Me, too."

"Especially if his hair comes in red."

"Floyd's momma prays against that happenin' every day."

At lower speeds the truck grumbled and lurched awkwardly at times. In the bottoms beside the river lay the best growing dirt in the region. The houses near these unshapely stretching fields were burly and flush, with young trucks in the driveways and paid-off tractors in the barns. Chopped cornstalks poked above the snow, and useless old tassels and shucks had blown into the wire fencerows and stuck to the barbs.

Coyotes began calling down the moon.

Ree held Ned tugged to her side and said, "Let's get on home. This is no good. I mean, why would he be runnin' if he saw me wavin'?"

WHERE REE slept the night shadows seemed never to change. A yard light across the creek cast a beam at the same angle as always through her frosted window. She sat up in bed listening to *The Sounds of Tranquil Streams* while watching the same old shadows and vanishing sprites of her own boring breath. She raised two quilts and draped them across her shoulders while the stream tumbled chanting around a rocky bend and she considered forever and how shadowed and lonely it would likely be.

In Ree's heart there was room for more. Any evening spent with Gail was like one of the yearning stories from her sleep was happening awake. Sharing the small simple parts of life with someone who stood tall in her feelings. She stretched flat and turned the knob to quiet the stream. Counseled by midnight and a clutched pillow she eventually eased into sleep.

Knocking sounds pulled her awake. There was no radiant heat this far from the stove and she stood on the cold wood of the floor and looked out the window and saw the antique truck. The frigid air raised bumps on her skin as she went toward the knocking.

Gail said, "He told me if I was goin' to stay out *this* late, I might as well stay out *all night*. He took Ned to his folks'n shut the door on me."

Ree waved her inside and threaded through the dark to bed and crawled yawning under the heavy quilts. Gail sat on a chair and began to undress. Her breathing floated welcome ghosts into the air. Caked mud broke loose when boots thumped to the floor. Jeans and socks were dropped in a bunch on top of the boots. She fidgeted on bare feet and rubbed at the skin of her shoulders and arms, looking down at the bed.

Ree held the quilts pulled wide, patted the sheet, and said, "One log alone won't hold fire."

THE NEEDED skill was silence. Along the dangle of knotted branches gray squirrels crouched utterly still as the day roused. They were alarmed by every sound but not long alarmed by any. The dawn air held the cold of night but there was no breeze and squirrels soon lost their fear of the new day and moved out along the branches. Easy meat for the table with naught but silence and a small bullet required.

Ree and the boys sat with their backs propped against a large fallen oak, butts on gathered leaves, boots in thin patches of snow. Trees were yet in shadow down low but fresh sunlight warmed the upper reaches. Ree noted a squirrel standing upright on a high sunny branch and slowly raised the rifle and popped a shot. The squirrel squeaked mortally and spun a loop on the branch, hind claws scraping at bark for a final grip before falling limp to ground. Harold budged forward to retrieve the squirrel but Ree held him back. She shook her head and whispered, "Leave him lay. They all run into their holes hearin' that shot, but if you stay still'n quiet they'll come right back out in a few minutes. We want two more."

She passed the rifle to Sonny, and they leaned back to wait. The boys had red noses and Ree told them with gestures not to sniffle their snot but to let it build full, then remove it with one quick snort. Sonny saw a squirrel lying along a thick branch but fired too low and splattered bark chips. He frowned and passed the rifle to Harold. The sun rose and tree shadows began stretching wide across the open spaces. Harold's shot did not hit squirrel or tree, a wasted bullet sent whirring into the distance. Ree pegged another and Harold winced as the squirrel fell squeaking and clawing feebly at the air. This one bounced off several branches and landed on a log. With his next shot Sonny hit his target in the hind parts and the squirrel thudded to ground and started to scramble awkwardly in the snow and winter brambles.

Ree nudged Harold. "You can chase after that one. They got claws'n teeth, you know, so wear gloves to grab 'em."

"He's still alive!"

"Notch his head 'tween two fingers'n pull — like with a chicken."

"He's callin' for his momma!"

Sonny stood and shook feeling into his legs, then slipped on his yellow leather gloves and walked toward the maimed squirrel thrashing about in snow spotting with blood.

"I'll do it — he's mine, anyhow."

The squirrel huffed after breath and squeaked things defiant or pitiful or both. Sonny hunkered and dropped a hand over the squirrel's little head and jerked it beyond connection with the body though the skull remained inside the fur. He watched the chest sink a last time, then gathered the others and carried them all by their tails.

Ree said, "There's a way to make a stringer for these things if you get a big bunch. These bones here, behind this thing like an ankle? You can poke a hole there between the bones and run a stringer through like with fish, but we don't need a stringer today. Not for this amount."

Harold said, "Let me carry one."

The sun was taller though light had not yet broken through to the ground. The path was narrow and iced on the north slope. These rough acres were Bromont acres and they'd never been razed for timber, so the biggest old trees in the area stood on this ground. Magically fat and towering oak trees with limbs grown into pleasingly akimbo swirls were common. Hickory, sycamore, and all the rest prospered as well. The last stretch of native pine in the county grew up the way, and all the old-growth timber was much coveted by sneaking men with saws. If sold, the timber could fetch a fair pile of dollars, probably, but it was understood by the first Bromont and passed down to the rest that the true price of such a sale would be the ruination of home, and despite lean years of hardship no generation yet wanted to be the one who wrought that upon the family land. Grandad Bromont had famously chased timber-snakers away at gunpoint many, many times, and though Dad had never been eager to wave his gun about in defense of trees, he'd loaded up and done it whenever required.

Sonny said, "Look — I can stick my little finger down inside the hole. It sticks down purty deep, too."

"Don't you go lickin' that finger, now."

"I think I feel the bullet."

They crested the slope, breakfast held swinging by the tail, and started toward the house below. Smoke drifted from the stack. Across the creek a cussing Milton was trying to start a cold balky truck while another Milton banged on the motor with a wrench. Ree kept her eyes on her side of the creek and led the boys down the curving damp trail to the rear of the house.

Harold said, "Ree, are these for fryin' or for stewin'?"

"Which way do you like best?"

Both boys said, "Fried!"

"Okey-doke. Fried, then. With biscuits, maybe, if we got the makin's, and spang dripped on top, too. But, first thing is, we got to clean 'em. Sonny, you fetch the skinnin' board. I think it's still leanin' on the side of the shed back there. Harold, you go for the knife — you know which one I want."

"The one I ain't s'posed to never touch."

"Bring it to me."

The skinning board was a weathered barn slat scored with a snarl of cuts and stained by various bloods. Sonny laid the board at Ree's feet and she dropped one squirrel onto the wood and set the others to the side. When Harold returned with the knife, Gail came with him and stood on the porch, sipping coffee.

Ree said, "Hey, Sweet Pea, how'd you sleep?"

"Good as ever."

Sonny nudged Ree with his elbow, said, "Show me how, huh?"

"I'll show the both of you — Harold, you stay close."

She stretched the squirrel lengthwise and drove the blade in at the neck.

"Now, these are harder'n rabbits but still not too hard, really. Think like you're cuttin' the squirrel a suit, only you're cuttin' the suit *off* of 'em, not for 'em to put on. Open 'em at the neck, here, cut the wrists free like so and slit the arms, cut the ankles free like so and slit the legs, then split 'em like this down the middle and bring all the cuts together. Their skin sticks to 'em more than rabbits, so you got to pull at it, and help it along by easin' the blade between the fur and the meat. Harold, put your hand in there'n yank out them guts."

"I ain't touchin' guts!"

"Don't be scared — the thing's dead. Nothin' to be scared of."

Harold backed slowly toward Gail and onto the porch.

"I ain't *scared* to do it, I just don't *want* to do it."

Sonny crouched to the skinning board and shoved his fist inside the squirrel and pulled the guts onto the wood. He scrunched his face and shook his head. The guts made a somber pile of deep reds and pale reds, browns, and blacks. He looked at the guts, then at Harold. He said, "It ain't no worse'n cleanin' up puke or somethin'. You should do the next one."

"But cleanin' up puke always makes *me* puke."

Ree was watchful over Sonny as he split the next squirrel

open. She said, "You got you a whole bunch of stuff you're goin' to have to get over bein' scared of, boy."

Gail said, "Harold, you got the sand for this, ain't you?" She stroked his dark hair and when his eyes met hers she bent to kiss his cheek. He blushed, leaned his head into her middle, and threw an arm around her waist. "I've always known you to be such a brave little rascal."

"You can't always leave all the ugly stuff to Sonny, you know. That ain't right."

"I don't mind — he's my only brother."

"I mind. Harold, get your butt down here. You don't wanna make me run after you. You truly don't. Get down here now'n squat beside me. Close your eyes if you want, but get your goddam fingers in there'n yank out them guts."

Harold did not move and Ree stood to grab him by a wrist. She pulled him down the porch steps to the skinning board. He crouched on his knees with his eyes held shut and she guided his hand inside the squirrel. He made the sort of face that generally breaks into tears, but squeezed with his hand and pulled and pulled until the guts lay on the board. He stood then, calmly looked at his hand, then at the guts. He said, "That really *ain't* no biggie, is it? His insides sure was good'n warm on my fingers."

Gail said, "Look at Harold! Look who's still the brave, brave little rascal I always thought he was."

Harold seemed embarrassed but pleased and stood over the gut piles staring down. "We don't never eat those parts, anyhow, do we?"

"Nope."

Sonny and Harold rushed together beaming then and slapped their bloody hands at each other. They stood still giggling for a moment and carefully rolled red fingers across each other's cheeks to make spotty war paint stripes. They laughed and hopped about the snow-caked yard, swatting away with bloody hands while Ree tossed the remaining squirrel onto the skinning board and bent to cut the suit.

FULL STOMACHS brought about a spell of peace and Ree languished on the couch. She stretched on her back with her long legs propped atop the armrest and put a dish towel over her eyes so the pictures playing inside her head would flicker brightly against a darkened space. A tiny purple circle puffed into a large blue circle, an expanding bucket mouth, maybe, and inside the bucket it was like ten gazillion fireflies popped into sparks but their sparking light was of all the colors known to the mind and constantly popping from one color into another. A red cloud of mist grew from the bucket and shrunk into a regular little crooked tree on a hilltop with an old wrinkled sky above. When the wrinkles parted the sky was a blue eye that winked until she was in the tree with her feet hanging from a branch, dangling above a sudden roiling ocean that opened below. The ocean had waves that leapt like dancers. A smattering of cows grazed between dancers in the ocean but many others puffed with bloat and floated foundering horribly on their sides just beyond reach of the waves until pitchfork tines swooping down from somewhere pierced their bloated bellies all at once and the released fart-wind from so many bloated cows knocked her flying from the tree into a fragile green jungle. The jungle shattered into smoke behind her as she ran and held people she knew, sort of, at least she sensed that she did, but they wouldn't face her or say hello or stop to help with directions. All her feelings were of being lost and her frantic words were shouted in a language nobody else seemed to hear. She ducked under a yellow leaf big as tomorrow and fell against giant time-spanning lips that could smooch her spirit entire from days of girlhood to now with but one knowing pucker. The lips kept smooching on her sweetly like she was yet and forever a child, though, which felt wrong, stunting and stale, then in the measure of a single heartbeat her dress fell open like shutters and she stood revealed, a woman, and . . .

The dish towel fell from her eyes and the flickering pictures sank beneath light with the lips sinking away last, even as she felt her fingers reach out to grab them for holding near. She opened her eyes to see Uncle Teardrop's face poised inches above her own, and seen at this distance his melted side looked as big as a continent on a globe. He said, "You think I forgot about you?"

It was a continent with a volcanic history, vast sections of wasteland and rugged brown mountainous zones rained upon eternally by three blue drops. Her eyes took it all in as she rolled off the couch sideways beneath him onto her knees and hurried across the floor. As she crawled she said, "What do you mean, forgot about me? Huh?"

Uncle Teardrop wore a brown leather jacket that had been slashed open in a couple of places and home-stitched back

together with fat leather strands, and a camouflage cap meant
for green seasons. His dark graying hair was dull, lank. His
black jeans had washed pale in patches and his boots were dun
lace-ups. There'd be a weapon on him somewhere.

"Forgot about you and everything happenin' over here."

She stood near the far window and avoided his eyes.

"That's your business — forget us if you want."

He turned to look calmly her way while giving a slight
shake of his head.

"Jessup never would smack you. I don't know why, why he
never would, but I always have said someday somebody's
goin' to pay a price for him not whompin' you good when
you needed it."

Gail was napping in Ree's bed, the boys ran loudly about
in the side yard, and Mom sat silently in her rocker. Ree
edged along the wall so there'd be furniture blocking his way
if he made a mean move toward her.

"I wasn't tryin' to be a smart mouth, there, Teardrop.
Uncle Teardrop."

"It don't seem like you've got to try none, girl, smarty-
mouth shit just flies out your yap anytime your yap falls
open." He walked to the window that overlooked the side
yard. Sonny and Harold chased each other around in circles,
flinging snowballs while yelling fantastic threats back and
forth. Teardrop stood with his arms crossed and studied their
play like he was scouting the boys for the future. He was silent
long enough for the quiet to become worrisome to Ree,
then said, "He's faster'n Blond Milton ever was. He hits stuff
he throws at, too. Blond Milton, he always was strong as stink

but he threw rocks'n balls'n shit about like an ol' granny would without her glasses on, and he never could swim real swift or play horseshoes worth a damn or whatever. He wasn't coordinated as Sonny is already at any of that. Course, the man has proved he'll *shoot* anybody he wants, and not everybody will." He leaned to the window as he watched the boys a moment longer, eyes following them as they moved, until he eventually grunted once, shrugged his shoulders. "Harold, though. Harold better like guns." He pulled away from the window and turned about. "The law found Jessup's car out at Gullett Lake this mornin'. Somebody set it on fire last night, burnt it down to nothin' almost."

"Was . . . ?"

"He wasn't in it."

Late-morning shadows worked patterns across the scarred wooden floor, patterns underfoot shifting angle and design at the pace of the sun crossing the sky. Mom's eyes fell closed as though she'd heard and she began to hum a short snatch of flat music that nearly brought a song to mind. Teardrop's green truck was down in the yard and the boys ran around it hurling dripping snowballs at each other. Ree felt a low vibration become electric in the jelly between her bones and heart, and said, "He's gone, ain't he?"

"This is for you-all." Teardrop took a flat square of folded dollars from inside his jacket and tossed it to the couch. "His court day was this mornin' and he didn't show." He flung his arm out, gesturing vaguely toward the land up the hill behind the house. "I'd sell off that Bromont timber now while you can."

"No, huh-uh. I won't be doin' nothin' like that."

"That's the very first thing they'll do once they've took this place from under you-all, girl. Go up'n cut them woods down to nubs." He stepped to stand before her and put a hand beneath her chin, raised her eyes to meet his. "Might as well have the dough to spend on your own." He stood back, plucked a bag of crank from the smoke pocket on his shirt, scooped a load with a long fingernail and snorted, snorted again. He twisted his neck while rubbing his nose and the black dots in his eyes burst wider and darker. He held the bag to Ree. "You got the taste for it yet?"

"Hell, no."

"Suit yourself, little girl." He rolled the bag, put the crank away, turned in a circle to inhale the room, stopped suddenly to stare directly at Mom, humming with her eyes closed. He squinted and listened to her disjointed song awhile before turning from her. "She ain't moved since I was here in April." He walked to the front door and opened it, then turned to look at Mom again. "This floor, here? I remember when this floor here used to get to jumpin' like a fuckin' bunny from all the dancin'. Everybody dancin' around all night, stoned out of their minds — and it always was the happy kind of stoned back then."

Ree held the door open and leaned against the jamb to see him leave. She felt blue and ruined, as adrift and puny as an ash flake caught in a tossing wind. Teardrop started his green truck and gunned the engine until it roared, then turned around to head out. The boys stood together beside the rut road to watch him go by, stood a little bit scared and very still, their arms hanging at their sides, faces empty of any telling expression. Uncle Teardrop eased the truck slowly, slowly alongside them, stared at them intently without a word of greeting or gesture of recognition, and with no change in speed drove out of sight.

MOM STOOD when asked and Ree dressed her in a white winter coat that was puffy and slick and a yellow stocking hat that had a floppy yellow ball knit at the peak. Ree opened the side door and ushered her outside into the yard. Mom seldom left the house and her face looked anxious. She stepped uncertainly onto the thin snow, first tapping about with a toe before letting her heel come down. Ree held her by the elbow and led her to the steep trail on the north slope. The sun was dropping behind the far ridges, and in such light ice on the trail looked like spilled milk frozen hard.

After each step up the trail Mom would pause and lean back on Ree until Ree boosted her forward again. The routine acquired a working rhythm when Ree began boosting Mom along in that brief second before her pause could become a lean. Brittle ice snapped as boots fell and toes pressed forward. Mom's breath washed back in gusts to break across Ree's face. The warmth and flavor of Mom's breath held sweetness and opened memories. Mom before she was all the way crazy, lolling with Ree on a blanket between the pines, telling windy tales of whiffle-birds, the galoopus, the bingbuffer, and other Ozark creatures seldom seen in these woods but known for generations to live there. The whiffle-bird, a jolly feathered mystery just waiting to be born from shadows hatching to spark aloft quick as thought and fly backwards like a riddle across the sky, or the galoopus that might come roost deep down your well and lay perfectly square eggs of stiff yellow taffy inside your water bucket, or the taunting spooky bingbuffer that would creep close on the darkest of dark stormy nights to flex a huge hinged tail and peg rocks banging against your house while you pulled the blankets over your head and waited for the sun. Mom's words had tickled and her close breaths had soothed.

At the crest they began to walk gingerly through the Bromont acres. Ree linked arms with Mom and steered a course between stout trunks, carefully stepping over thick roots and blurs of ice. They walked near the rim of the knob and could see distant spots in the valley while heavy trees loomed over their shoulders. A band of crows sat on limbs high above and gabbed as the women passed below. The knob was bare slab rock in some spots, and the slab rocks were yet too slickery to walk across. Ree moved between gray slabs, squeezing with her arm to prompt Mom in one direction or another. At a breakneck bluff above a wet-weather creek they paused to stare to the next knob over, where the first Bromont house had been built. The walls and such had been carted away long ago but the square rock foundation still gave a base of ordered shapeliness to the barrage of runt oak and creeper vines that had overgrown the place.

Ree turned to walk along the north slope and up into the pines. Mom tripped on a root and slipped to her knees, and her expression jolted almost alert. She said, "How long has this snow been here?"

"Days and days now."

"I saw when it came."

Beneath the pines the ground was kept clear by falling needles, a soft carpet of browned needles spread under the low branches, a natural rumpus space for short scampering youngsters. The pines could easily be imagined into a castle or a sailing ship or serve merely as an ideal picnic spot. The trees broke any wind that came and lent a good scent to any season.

Mom held on to a branch and paused. "This is where I used to play."

"Me, too."

"Plus Bernadette."

Ree pulled Mom snug to her side, walked between the pines, the sharp needles and swishing branches, then downhill and across the wet-weather creek to the next wooded mound. There were footprints in the snow, raccoons and rabbits and a pair of coyotes that had prowled near for a sniff. Ree pulled Mom along uphill into the dense hardwood. Many pauses were required, and deep sucks of air, before the crest was reached. The trees were large and august and faithful. A huge oak stump sawed level made a sitting place overlooking the valley. The stump had become frayed and squishy from rot but made a wide pleasant seat.

Mom sat and Ree sat beside her. Ree held Mom's hand a moment, then came off the stump to kneel. She squeezed with both hands and tilted her face to look up at Mom.

"Mom, I need you. Mom — look at me. Look at me, Mom. Mom, I'm goin' to need you to help. There's things happenin' that I don't know what to do about. Mom? Look at me, Mom. Mom?"

The going sun chucked a vast spread of red behind the ridgeline. A horizon of red light parsed into shafts by standing trees to throw pink in streaks across the valley snow.

Ree waited kneeling for several minutes, kneeling as raised hopes fell to modest hopes, slight hopes, vague hopes, kneeling until any hope at all withered to none between her pressing hands. She released Mom, stood and walked away into the shadows behind the stump. She returned in a minute and looked closely at her from above, then sat on the stump again. Mom's skin was sallow, her face was blank and her soul was sincerely given over to silence and the approximate refuge offered by incomprehension. Mom stared into the sunset, then pulled her knees to her chest and wrapped her arms around herself and held tight.

"Mom?"

During the next minutes Ree leaned to look into her face a few times. Mom's gaze stayed unwaveringly on the glowing distance, chin to her kneecaps, hands clasped around her shins. Ree scooted away on the old stump and studied Mom's face in profile, the rounding features and sagged cheeks, then sighed and looked west. Sunlight shriveled to a red dot beyond the ridge, night swallowed the dot in a gulp, and the vista quickly began to sink from sight. Ree stood, pulled Mom to her feet, and arm in arm they started the darkened walk downhill to home.

FLOYD CAME by after dark with the baby. Gail had at least three times since noon told Ree her breasts ached a little and she latched onto Ned like he was medicine and carried him to the couch. She sat back, opened up in a hurry and gave him a nipple he seemed eager to get. Ree sat in a chair by the far window and tried not to listen to the husband and wife talk, but she heard it all. Floyd wanted Gail home, his momma couldn't keep up with a kid Ned's age and the trailer was too quiet without the noise of her cooing at the boy, goo-goo-gooing and all. Plus her catalogue had come in the mail and she could page around and pick out something pretty for springtime and he'd likely get it for her. Gail switched Ned to the other nipple and seemed to feel less ache drop by drop. She said some shit had to change. He ain't the boss of her every minute of every day. He said okay. But the big deal is that goddam Heather — you've got to quit fuckin' Heather. Floyd didn't say a word. Sonny and Harold slunk up close to see the tit the baby sucked, and the baby sucking was the only sound. Floyd lit a cigarette, then got to his feet and went outside. Gail bounced the baby, saying, *There, there.*

There, there. The door opened and Floyd set down a black suitcase and the blue bag of baby stuff, then stepped backwards and pulled the door shut. Both boys leaned on the couch arm staring at Gail's breasts and the headlight beams from Floyd's truck swept across the window glass as he drove away. Ree went over behind the couch and began rubbing Gail's neck. *There, there. He'll be back. He'll be back to get you again, most likely on laundry day, I bet. He'll be sayin' ol' Heather has got fat and sour of a sudden, she truly has, and god but he misses you sore. Come on home, sweetheart — soap's under the sink.* What Gail said was, *At least he didn't try to lie this time. Did you notice?*

REE PUSHED a mulish shopping cart in the Bawbee Store, with Ned in the basket and Gail beside her. Ned slept and slobbered bubbly while she and Gail shopped as a pair. The wheels were splayed like walleyes, so the cart would not easily go where it looked to be aimed but screeched off-line in half-moon spins toward one side of the aisle, then the other. Ree hunched forward and rode the cart like she was plowing a crooked row, holding hard and muscling the thing more or less where she wanted to go. She put noodles, rice and dried beans into the cart. She had already dropped in cans of soup, tomato sauce and tuna, a full chub of bologna, three loaves of bread, two boxes each of oatmeal and grits, plus three family packs of ground beef. She paused to stare at her load, finger at her lips, then put the rice back on the shelf and grabbed more noodles. She said, "I don't know what he done was wrong. Not for sure."

Gail said, "With all them noodles you'll want sprinkle cheese, won't you?"

"It costs too much for what you get. So we always skip it."

"Either he stole or he told. Those are the things they kill you for."

"I can't see Dad squealin'. Dad didn't have no dog in him."

"This generic here don't cost much."

"Naw, skip it."

"It tastes just about the same."

"Nope. Once the boys start likin' it they'll want it all the time. It's too expensive. It costs even more'n meat does."

"Oh, man," Gail said, "it just hit me — I must've been raised up rich — we *always* had sprinkle cheese."

Ree laughed and draped an arm across Gail's shoulders. "But you turned out okay, anyhow, Sweet Pea. The sugar-tit life ain't spoiled you none. None that I can see."

Gail tossed two canisters of sprinkle cheese into the cart, saying, "I'll buy those on my nickel." She reached to the opposite shelf and grabbed a can. "Plus these tamales."

The morning sun polished the hard road to a blinding sheen and both girls squinted on the way to the house. Mud holes were growing brown spots in the blanket of snow. The holes held water and birds pecked in the mud. A couple of saplings had roots spring loose in the wet and had fallen partway onto the road, and the thin ends of branches crunched under the truck tires.

While on the rut road to the house Ree looked across the creek. Blond Milton and Catfish Milton were standing by the bridge with a stranger. There was a parked white car that had a long antenna raised from the trunk. Both Miltons and the stranger watched the truck come along the rut. The stranger pointed, shrugged, started walking across the bridge.

Ree said, "Who the fuck is he?"

Gail said, "Somebody from town — look at the pretty shoes he's got on!"

Ree hefted groceries while Gail hefted Ned. Both of them stopped on the porch and turned to the stranger. Ree set her sacks down, said, "That'll do, mister. Right there. What is it you want?"

The man stood tall inside his thick coat, a hide and wool sheep coat with wide fuzzy lapels. He might've been thirty years old and wore mirror sunglasses and a leg holster. His Adam's apple was big and jumpy in his throat, brown hair fell thick to his shoulders. Two inches of whiskers drooped from the point of his chin. He looked like he meant no harm but could do plenty if pushed, and said, "I'm Mike Satterfield, from Three X Bail Bonds. We hold the bond on Jessup Dolly, and he's now a runner, it looks like."

"Dad ain't a runner."

"He didn't show for court — that makes him a runner."

"Dad's dead. He didn't show in court 'cause he's out layin' dead somewhere."

Satterfield stopped at the bottom of the steps, removed his sunglasses. His eyes were hazel and calm but interested. He leaned sideways against the handrail while looking at Ree.

"That ain't what I want to hear. It surely ain't. That's no good for nobody, none of us. You understand I've got the legal right to search anywhere I want in this place huntin' the man? I mean, I can go on in there if I want, check the closets'n attic, poke under beds'n stuff. You know that, kid?"

"I know you'd be wastin' your time if you did. Wastin' your time'n pissin' me off is all you'd be doin'." Gail stepped inside with Ned, and Ree came down the steps. "How long do I got? How long before we get thrown out?"

"Well, that depends on if I can find him and drag him back."

"Look, man, listen to me, it's like this — *Jessup Dolly is dead*. He is in a crappy little grave or become piles of shit in a hog pen or has busted to bits tossed down a deep cave hole. Maybe he was left out plain in the open and is rottin' away in a snow pile nobody has looked under yet, but, wherever, he's dead, man."

Satterfield shook a cigarette from a pack, lit up and exhaled. He had the habit of swatting his long hair from his face with the back of a hand. He said, "And you know this how?"

"You must've heard about what Dollys are, ain't you, mister?"

"Only all my life. I mean, I always have heard what *some* are, anyway. I imagine most everybody for a hundred miles round here has."

"Well, I'm a Dolly, bred'n buttered, and that's how I know Dad's dead."

He looked across the creek at the watchful Miltons, nodded.

"Those fellas're kin, of course, right? They wouldn't say boo to me, neither one, even though my dad has written bonds on the both of them, too, over the years. The idea I got from them was they didn't know no Jessup Dolly, or anybody that matched that description." He smoked while looking closely at Ree. "This thing has felt a little funny from the giddy-up. Smelled just a tad bit off. This house'n stuff of you-all's didn't cover the man's bond, not nearly — you know that?"

"Nobody told me nothin'. I found out everything after."

"Well, he was short on the bond, but a fella come into the office one evening, had a plastic sack of crinkled money and put it down to cover the rest. When I went over there to the jail, your dad didn't seem a hundred percent sure he even *wanted* out of lockup, neither, which ain't usually how they act, but he was sprung by breakfast. It seemed like somebody needed him sprung in a hurry."

"He was a good crank cook."

"So I've heard. Maybe that was it, they needed some batches run and wanted him for it."

Ree said, "This fella with the money have a name?"

"Nope. He must've left it in his other pants."

"What'd he look like?"

Satterfield glanced around the yard, up at the house, up the hill to the timber, said, "The plastic sack of cash is all I recall, kid." He dropped his cigarette to the snow, rubbed it with the sharp glossy toes of his pretty town shoes. "You probly got this place about another thirty days, kid. That's my guess."

There was a sound in Ree's head like a world of zippers zipping shut, and a sudden tilt factor engaged every place she looked. The creek shifted heights in her eyes and swayed overhead floppy as snapped string, the houses beyond warped skinny as ribs and knotted together in bows, the sky spun upright like a blue plate set on edge to dry. She had a feeling within of tipping over, tipping over somehow to dribble down and away, down and away bleakly to a place beyond reach.

She lunged at Satterfield, grasped the fuzzy lapels on his sheep coat, tugged.

"That's it? That's it? There ain't *nothin'* I can do?"

He pried her fingers loose, stepped backwards.

"No. No, I don't think there's nothin' left to do." He swatted his hair a couple of times, then began walking slowly toward the bridge, carefully placing his steps between snow and mud. He stopped at the bridge and stared at the clear water below running south, then turned back to her. "Nothin' unless you can *prove* he's dead. That'd sure 'nough turn things around. Dead men can't be expected to show in court."

Ree stood there wobbling in her soul until Satterfield reached his car. She turned to go up the porch steps with her thoughts twirling and saw Gail standing in the open doorway with her arms crossed. From inside came clanging voices as the boys excitedly examined the rich plunder of groceries, slamming cans into the cupboard, loudly staking claim to favored foods. Gail's face pinched with concern so the freckles seemed to gather in a blot, and her eyes were narrowed. She said, "I heard that last thing he said, Sweet Pea, and *don't you do it.* I know the way you are, how you go about things, and I'm sayin', *don't you go back there.*"

Across the creek the white car began to move, pulled onto a mudflat between houses and circled about in a hurry to leave. Mud sprayed from the rut to daub the front porches.

Ree fell as much as sat to the top step, knees wide, chin down, and said, "How else is it goin' to happen?"

R EE WALKED down the Hawkfall hill with nothing watching her back but the sun. She kicked her boots scuffing loudly along the road and looked at thin smoke rails rising from chimneys below. Twice she turned about to stare toward home, but the antique truck was already beyond sight. Snow piles still lined the road, melting, but the fields were fast becoming mud acres with tattering white borders. Cows walking near the fenceline made sucking sounds as each hoof was pulled from the holding mud. Pouring sunlight rubbed the cowhides shiny and raised sweat on Ree's face. Mamaw's coat felt too heavy in the turning weather but she kept it on all the way down the slope and into the meadow of old fallen walls.

Disappearing snow left the old tossed stones plain amidst the puny winter weeds and spreading muck. Some stones were stacked two high and some lay in close clusters with stunted oak growing from the narrow spaces between. Cows had been grazed in the meadow and they'd walked bare paths into the grass and around the stones. Here and there small pieces of shattered stained glass glinted surprise colors from the cow-path mud.

The drive up to Thump Milton's house was wide enough for two cars to pass and coated with pea gravel. The gravel gave way underfoot so that each step sounded like a shovel digging. Trees lined the drive and many birds sang from the limbs but their songs were not the same. Near the dun house there were two cars and two trucks parked. A redbone hound resting in a truck bed stood as she approached and barked.

The house door opened and Mrs. Thump looked out. She closed the door briefly, then came outside carrying a steaming cup. Mams hung to the belly of her stout frame and heaved as she advanced. Two other women stepped onto the porch behind Mrs. Thump and both had postures and chins that suggested they were her close relatives. Mrs. Thump's white hair was done up in big pink rollers held in place by a mostly yellow scarf.

Ree reached for the steaming cup, smiling, and said, "I'm not really—" And the world flushed upside down in her eyes while her ears rang and she staggered, then the world flushed again and again and she stumbled across the gravel. One of Mrs. Thump's rollers had jerked loose and dangled springy around her head as she pulled her big hand back to whack Ree another in the face, and Ree swung a fist at those blunt teeth in a red mouth but missed. The other women closed in with boots to the shins while more heavy whacks landed and

Ree felt her joints unglue, become loose, and she was draining somehow, draining to the dirt, while black wings flying angles crossed her mind, and there were the mutters of beasts uncaged from women and she was sunk to a moaning place, kicked into silence.

WORDS WERE reaching her but none that she understood. The pain was dense and dazzling and traveled her body in pounding waves. It had been only black in her spirit until small slices of dull light began creeping toward the center of awareness from the rim, but her first brightened thoughts were jumbled and ungraspable. There were shovels, she heard shovels, several shovels digging around her, then she was hefted aloft and flying along in agony until crashed to a new ground that smelled of straw and feed sacks. She screamed landing. Her ears hummed ugly noise and her nose felt thickened. She tasted blood, spit marbles to the straw. Her tongue moved along the slick in her mouth to a leaking vacancy where two teeth had been.

"She's crazy to've come here — wouldn't you say that means she's crazy?"

Only one eye would open.

"Her momma's crazy, so there's a good shot of her bein' crazy, too."

The women stood over her, spires of menace wearing

lipstick and scarves. They saw her eye open and she sat up, aching in her ribs, her legs, her everywhere. Her teeth lay dirty in the straw, broken from her mouth, cap and root, and she stretched their way, fumbled both onto a palm, made a fist around them. She mumbled, "I ain't crazy. I ain't crazy." She spluttered blood and dropped her teeth into a pocket of Mamaw's coat. Her words were wounded in her mouth, crippled in shape but flung hard as a dying wail. *"And I ain't never goin' to be crazy, neither!"*

Mrs. Thump stepped closer, into plain view, with her hair rolled back into place beneath a snug scarf. She seemed grim and unruffled.

"You was warned. You was warned nice'n you wouldn't listen — why didn't you listen?"

"I *can't* listen. I can't *just* listen."

She moved her head slowly, wobbling as she aimed her good eye, and saw that there were others in the barn. Shapes milling by the open double door, wearing man hats, smoking, watching in silence. One of the man hats stepped near. Megan squatted, patted Ree's face, and said, "Whatever are we to do about you, baby girl? Huh?"

"Kill me, I guess."

"That idea has been said already. Got'ny other ones?"

"Help me. Ain't nobody said that idea yet, have they?"

The sightless eye was fattened shut and stretched tight. She felt the swelling and tried to pry the eyelid open, but could not even sense daylight through that eye. Blood had to be spit and came out in heavy wads trailed by stringy drools that lapped onto her chin and cheeks. With her tongue she could feel shreds of her own meat broken from inside her lips. Her skirt was thrown up and her legs were decked with bruises that colored uglier as she watched.

Megan said, "I tried to help you some the other day, and this is what come of that."

Near the door the small crowd began to part, make way, and though nobody spoke his name, Ree knew Thump Milton had come into the barn. Ree could tell a hatted shape was stepping toward her, a shape wearing an olden sort of farmer's winter cap with stretch earflaps and a stovepipe crown. Megan glanced at the advancing hat, then stood and quickly moved aside.

Thump Milton loomed over Ree, a fabled man, his face a monument of Ozark stone, with juts and angles and cold shaded parts the sun never touched. His spade beard was aged gray but his movements were young. He crouched, grabbed her chin, and turned her head from side to side, inspecting the damage. He was bigger than she'd thought, hands strong as stormwater rushing. His eyes went inside you to the depths without asking and helped themselves to anything they wanted.

He said, "You got somethin' you need to say, child, you best say it now."

His voice held raised hammers and long shadows.

Ree could feel the sting of piss drying on her legs and a thicker expulsion mushed in her panties. There were pigeons watching from the rafters. Smells of sweat-soaked leather, spilled feed, and scared calves. Ree turned aside and vomited blood and lunch toward a slop bucket but spewed wide. When she looked up at Thump Milton, the women and the other hats from the doorway had come to stand close behind him. She recognized Little Arthur, Spider Milton, Cotton Milton, Buster Leroy, and one of the Boshell men, Sleepy John.

She spoke low with her head down, the words lamed by spatters of red wet and slow limping from her mouth. She said, "I got two little brothers who can't feed theirselves . . . yet. My mom is sick, and she is always . . . goin' to be sick. Pretty soon the laws're takin' our house away n'throwin' us out . . . to live in the fields . . . like dogs. Like fuckin' dogs. The only hope I got to keep our house is . . . is, I gotta *prove* . . . Dad's dead. Whoever killed him, I don't need . . . to know . . . that. I don't never need to know that. If Dad did wrong, Dad has paid. But I can't forever carry both . . . them boys'n Mom . . . not . . . without that house to help."

Her words were met with silence, an electric moment of utter silence, then Thump Milton stood and left the barn. Mrs. Thump and two of the men went with him. The others began to gather again near the doorway, whispering. Cigarettes were lit and funny things were said. The crowd chuckled at funny things she couldn't hear and there was a great ugly roaring in her ears. Megan moved on the fringe of the crowd, and twice it seemed like she might've nodded Ree's way.

Ree lay back on the barn floor, feeling the pitiful squish of her own voiding, and stared up. The pigeons in the rafters were awful quiet. Auction signs from long ago had been nailed to the underside of the hayloft floor and Ree stared at them but couldn't make the signs hold still long enough to read any of the items for sale. She felt rude swishing in her belly and rolled over to spew but didn't. Blood trickled from the side of her mouth to her earlobe and she wondered if Dad was lying on his side, too, or dead in a different position.

That redbone outside barked again, and a man in the doorway said, "Who's this comin' up here in such a big toot?"

Little Arthur said, "Is that truck green?"

"Looks green to me."

"Aw, shit — that's Teardrop's truck. Teardrop her fuckin' uncle — who the hell called him?"

The man said, "I don't know, but I gotta go quick get somethin' from my car. I ain't standin' here naked when that motherfucker walks in and sees her beat silly over there."

Ree sat up and one of the women took two steps toward her and hissed, "Now look what you did!"

The truck door slammed and she heard digging steps cross the pea gravel.

Little Arthur said, "Hey, Teardrop, what —"

"Where is she?"

"Don't get all excited."

"She in there?"

The women and the hatted men made way for Teardrop. He had his right hand jammed deep into the pocket of his slashed leather jacket. The sun came from behind so his face was blurred by his own shade. His head was bare and his eyes moved quickly through the crowd. He took a few steps toward Ree and abruptly stopped.

Little Arthur said, "She was told, man, and didn't listen."

Teardrop seemed to stand straighter as he looked at Ree but his expression did not change. His gaze lingered on her face, her legs, the fresh and drying blood threads crisscrossing her cheeks and chin and neck. He turned to Little Arthur, spread his feet.

"You hit her?"

Little Arthur draped an arm toward the small of his back. His shirt bunched as he put a hand to his belt. He said, "What'll you do if I did?"

"Say yes'n see."

Mrs. Thump stomped back into the barn and stepped up, waving her hands.

"He never! No man here touched that crazy girl!"

"No man did?"

"I drubbed her good myself."

Teardrop said, "You never drubbed her that way by yourself."

"Me and my sisters, they were here, too."

The crowd began to step aside and make way again, and Thump Milton returned to the barn. Buster Leroy and Sleepy John walked beside him and both carried shotguns, barrels pointed up, fingers near the triggers. Thump Milton strode forward with no hesitation to within an arm's length of Teardrop. His quick pace had stirred the barn dust and he stood in a billow of whirling motes. He looked directly into Teardrop's eyes and said, "Explain yourself, Haslam."

Teardrop stared back and did not truckle. He pointed with his left hand as he spoke. "I ain't never said a single fuckin' word about my brother. I ain't asked nobody about my brother, nor looked for him, neither. What Jessup done was against our ways, he knew it and I know it, and I ain't raised no stink at all about whatever became of him. *But she ain't my brother.* She's my niece, and she's near about all the close family I got left, so I'll be collectin' her now and carryin' her on out of here to home. That suit you, Thump?"

"You're willin' to stand for her, are you?"

"If she does wrong, you can put it on me."

"Agreed. She's now yours to answer for."

"This is a girl who ain't goin' to tell nobody nothin'."

A near wooden post looked useful and Ree crawled to it. The rough wood rasped on her hands as she pulled herself upright and everything she saw moved in slow circles. Moans droned from her chest of bones. Shit leaked from her panties and she felt runnels of yuck on her thighs. She fluffed her wadded skirt loose and down. She swayed on her feet and realized that Thump Milton and Uncle Teardrop had turned to watch her.

Thump Milton said, "Put the girl in Haslam's truck. Carry her if you got to." He faced Teardrop again and said, "Is this over now?"

Teardrop did not pull his eyes from Ree to address Thump Milton.

"If anybody lays even just one finger on that girl ever again, they better have shot me first."

Megan and Spider Milton put Ree between them and shouldered her from the barn. Her feet dragged up dust and pigeons flew from the eaves. The crowd was silent as she was hauled across the pea gravel to the green truck, but that red-bone barked once more and those birds in the trees still sang their different songs.

THERE WAS an echo in her eye. She looked from the speeding truck, and everything she saw — house, fence post, goat, cow, songbird, or shining sun — had an echo of itself standing at its side. The echoes all wavered a little, and if the real object moved the echo might fall behind and disappear from sight for a second or two before catching up again to stand close and make shimmering doubles in her eye.

Uncle Teardrop stared into the rearview mirror until the truck crested a hump and on the downside he slammed the brakes, then backed off the pavement onto a vague dirt path. He sped backwards across deep jarring ruts in a fallow field, past a fallen barn and into a thicket of dead apple trees. In the orchard he'd found darkness in daylight, a veiled space between rotting trees with a view of the road from Hawkfall.

He opened his door, stepped from the truck to bend and better reach under the seat. When he got back behind the wheel he held a paratrooper's rifle with a folding wire stock and a long clip, and a shotgun with the barrel cut short and a small white handgrip. He laid the shotgun beside Ree, tapped a finger on her knee, said, "For if they come." He leaned to her, turned her face up, and looked inside her mouth. He was sweating and his breaths were short. "That Gail girl really saved your bacon." He raised her shirttail, twisted the very end into a thick coil and stuck the coil into her mouth. "Put this where you're bleedin'n chomp down on it. Don't talk or nothin', just keep that thing chomped down good 'til the blood lets up."

She could sense blood driven by heartbeats pulsing from the torn places beneath her skin. She saw four eyes and two ears and a flurry of blue drops on Uncle Teardrop's face. She eased her hand toward the shotgun, located it by feel rather than by sight. She touched a finger to the cool barrel and clenched her jaw and nearly cried smelling the rising stink of herself.

Teardrop reached across to the glove box and grabbed a baby-food bottle of crank. He unscrewed the lid, set it on the dash, snorted from the bottle twice, banged the steering wheel, and said, "You got to be ready to die every day — then you got a chance." He sat in shade cast by the limbs of a dry orchard, staring toward the road. "You own me now. Understand? You purty much own me now, girl. You do wrong, it's on me. You do big wrong'n it's me that'll pay big. Jessup, he went'n did wrong, the poor silly shit. Jessup went'n turned snitch, and that's only the biggest ancient no-no of all, ain't it? I never thought . . . but he couldn't face this last bust, couldn't face a ten-year jolt. Plus there's your mom, sittin' home crazy forever. That was heavy on his mind. Them boys. You. He started talkin' to that fuckin' Baskin — but I want you to know, Jessup, Jessup wasn't givin' up *no Rathlin Valley* men. Huh-uh, huh-uh. He said he wasn't. Wouldn't do it. He said . . . shit, he said all kinds of . . . If I could do any of my days over, girl, that very first asshole I killed'd still be walkin' around. But . . . hell, never been found and I'm . . . You're forcin' me out into the open, girl. Understand? You're puttin' me into the exact picture I been tryin' to dodge. They been waitin' to see if I'll do anything. Watchin'. Listen . . . the way it is . . . the way I *feel* . . . is, I can't *know* who killed Jessup. I can suspicion a man or two, have a hinky feelin', but I can't *know* for a certain fact *who* went'n killed my little brother. Even if he did wrong, which he did, why . . . it'll eat at me if I know who they sent. Eat at me like red ants. Then . . . there'll come a night . . . a night when I have that one more snort I didn't need, and I'll show up somewhere'n see whichever fucker done it sippin' a beer'n hootin' at a joke and . . . shit . . . that'll be that. They'll all come for me then . . . Buster Leroy . . . Little Arthur . . . Cotton Milton, Whoop Milton, Dog . . . Punch . . . Hog-jaw . . . that droopy-eyed motherfucker Sleepy John. But, anyhow, girl, I'll help you some, take your back so you can find his bones, but the deal is, even if you find out, you *can't ever* let me know who did the actual killin' of my brother. Knowin' that'd just mean I'll be toes-up myself purty soon, too. Deal?"

Ree slid her hand from the shotgun barrel across the seat to Uncle Teardrop's arm, and squeezed, squeezed again. He turned his head away and started the engine. Dead limbs scraped the truck and broke to the ground. He drove out of the orchard and across the bumpy field to the road. He said, "You're a mess, let's get your ass home."

The world rippled in her view until she shut her eye and let her head loll to the window. Teardrop drove the dirt roads, the nigh cut to the house, and as the truck rattled down the rut he began to honk the horn. Ree opened her eye. He stopped just below the undulating porch with the shimmying rails and went around to open Ree's door. Gail jumped down the porch steps and ran with her echo to the truck and the boys echoed to a four-part stop in the doorway behind her. They appeared stunned to sickness by the sight of Ree's face. Gail instantly began to cry. She and Teardrop lifted Ree from the bench seat. Ree spit the stained coil from her mouth, rested her head on Gail, and whispered, "Help me wash. Burn my clothes. Please. Help me wash."

ALL HER aches were joined as a chorus to sing pain throughout her flesh and thoughts. Gail stood her straight and naked and cleaned her body as she would a babe's, using the soiled skirt to swab the spread muck from her ass and thighs and behind the knees. Gail touched her fingers to the revealed welts and bruises and shook between cries. When Ree moved she came loose and sagged as the chorus inside hit fresh sharp notes. Her agony was the song and the song held so many voices and Gail lowered her into the bathtub where sunk to her chin in tepid water she marked a slight hushing of all the chorus but the singers in her head.

THE WOMEN of Rathlin Valley began crossing the creek to view her even as she lay in the tub. Sonya led Betsy and Caradoc Dolly's widow, Permelia, who owned the third house in the rank of three on the far bank, into the bathroom and closed the door on the paled waiting boys with their stricken faces. Ree lay with her good eye open a peep in water skimmed thinly with suds. The women stood in a cluster looking down at the colored bruises on milk skin, the lumped eye, the broken mouth. Their lips were tight and they shook their heads. Permelia, ancient but mobile, witness to a hundred wounds, said, "There's never no call to do a girl like that."

Sonya said, "Merab's got a short fuse."

"Done booted her calico."

"Her sisters helped her."

Betsy, wife of Catfish Milton, gray young yet handsome, began to shudder with feeling. Betsy had never been chatty, but in the years since she'd lost her sweetest daughter to a tree limb that dropped on a calm blue day she could occasionally be heard in the night shouting threats from her yard at those shining stars that most troubled her. She knelt at the tub side, laid a flat palm on Ree's belly and rubbed a gentle circle, then stood trembling and fled the room.

The noise of boys sniffling in the parlor carried through the bathroom door.

Uncle Teardrop snapped, *Hush goddammit,* and they did.

Permelia said, "My say is, this is wrong. It can't ever be right to do a girl that way. Not between our own people."

Sonya said, "You can see three kinds of footprints stomped on her legs, there. Must've took them a while to track her up bad like that." She shook her head, then handed an orange plastic vial to Gail, and said, "Pain pills from Betsy's hysterectomy. Give her two to start."

"Just two?"

"She'll want more, but just two to start with, then build from there to whatever number lets her rest."

BY DUSK Ree had three kinds of pain pills sitting on the floor bedside next to her teeth. In her head she was furnishing a cave. Her teeth looked like some sort of baby tubers grown underground behind the shed and yanked out with stiff forked roots yet attached. Victoria came to sit at the foot of her bed and see her stomped so ugly with two teeth on the floor. Ree could feel the dunkle with her tongue. Victoria dwindled to a wan color and said things over her, or didn't, but left behind two kinds of Uncle Teardrop's pills and they swaddled her in warm pink clouds. Hauling the furniture up the slope would be the first hard part. Bunch of ropes'd be called for. Lay the beds in the middle room of the cave, maybe, in from the fire but not far. Boys here, Mom there. Take the table and chairs, both guns, Aunt Bernadette's dresser — or will the cave wet ruin good wooden things, bubble the veneer, warp drawers so they never open easy again?

Could be the good stuff ought to be sold.

Also, get teeth in town.

The boys crept to her side at early dark to sit around her,

mournful, with their heads bowed like they wished they knew how to pray the oldest prayers and pray her well. Harold held a cool cloth to her swollen eye. Sonny made fists and said, "What was the fight about?"

"Me bein' me, I guess."

"How many was it?"

"A few."

"Tell us the names. For when we grow up."

"I feel too good'n pink just now, boys. Let me drift."

A big-ass rug could be unrolled across the cave floor to smother dust and make smooth footing. Take the potbelly. Lanterns, clothesline, knives. Finish stacking rocks in the mouth. Pack all the thunder mugs and slide them under the beds. Something to cook on . . . can openers . . . hand soap . . . oh, man.

She slept into the darkest hours. She flinched asleep and tried to duck away from fists flying in her dreams. Knuckles out of darkness, boots that never shined, horrid grunts of women who felt righteous beating whatever they did. Thump's angled face and cold parts . . . the hats . . . Dad's body hung upside down from a limb to drain blood from his split neck into a black bucket.

I ain't never goin' to be crazy!

A golden fish in the bucket with a sparkling tail that swished bright words across the blood, bright words splashed past so fast they couldn't be understood, leaving the mind to guess at the words and just what the fish means by them and all those sparkles in blood.

I ain't never goin' to be crazy!

Gail says, "Sweet Pea, you want more pills? You're thrashin'."

"Okay. Make it the blue ones."

"There's no water."

"I gotta hit the john, anyhow."

"Here's two."

Ree stood and walked across the cold floor, walked slowly and bent. Moons of ache glowed in spaces of her meat and when she moved the moons banged together and stunned. When she sat on the stool all her stiffened places stretched open and loosed fresh hurt. She took the pills and drank from the tap with cupped hands, then shuffled back through the dark.

The rifle barrel made a shadow and she saw it before she saw the man. The man was on the couch, sitting by the window, and the rifle was propped against the arm. She felt he was watching her but she tried to become still as the darkness and blend anyhow. She forgot to breathe, until Uncle Teardrop spoke, "Get back to bed."

"What . . . 's goin' on?"

"I ain't big on trust, is what."

She sat on the far end of the couch. The potbelly door was ajar and by its dim glow she could see the heads of both boys, flat on the bed cushions, feet wiggled free of the blankets. She said, "I think I'll be okay. Not tomorrow or nothin', but sometime."

"You took that beatin' good as most men I've seen."

"Huh." Ree let her head fall back on the couch and closed her eye. She felt talkative from inside her pink cloud, chatty, maybe confessional. "What I really, really can't stand . . . is . . . is how I feel so shamed . . . for Dad. Snitchin' just goes against everything."

Wind rattled the windows in their frames. The yard light across the way glinted on old ice stuck to the panes. Mom snored short honking snores that carried. The smell of a filling ashtray hung in the air.

"Well, he loved y'all. That's where he went weak."

"But . . ."

"Listen, girl — lots of us can be tough, plenty tough enough, and do it for a long stretch, too." He pointed toward Mom's room, flung his arm out briskly and straight. "You know, Connie in there, Connie stood up plenty tough, too. She did. She really did. Stood tough through shootin's and prison bits for Jessup and all variety of shit before, I don't know why, but she sprung a leak and all her gumption leaked out."

"But snitchin' . . ."

"*Jessup wasn't always a snitch.* For lots'n lots of years he wasn't a snitch. He *wasn't,* and he *wasn't,* and he *wasn't,* then one day he was."

Ree looked to the potbelly and saw that Sonny sat up now, listening, his back to the wall, hearing words he'd be feeding on the rest of his life. She said, "That's why everybody sort of shuns us a little bit now, ain't it?"

A smell stretched from Uncle Teardrop, a sharp cooked stench like something electric had been plugged in too long and was burning out. He lit a smoke, leaned toward Ree, and in coming forward exposed his melted side to a faint spot of light. He said, "The Dollys around here can't be seen to coddle a snitch's family — that's always been our way. We're old blood, us people, and our ways was set firm long before hot-shot baby Jesus ever even burped milk'n shit yellow. Understand? But that shunnin' can change, some. Over time. Folks have noticed the sand you got, girl."

Ree watched as he smoked, watched and waited drowsily until he leaned backwards, unrolled a Baggie of crank, dipped a finger to the powder and snorted, gasped, snorted more. He sucked up hard with his nose. She yawned and said, "You always have scared me, Uncle Teardrop."

He said, "That's 'cause you're smart."

The blue pills bloomed inside Ree and suddenly made her droop in the darkness. She sagged drooling on the couch until Teardrop poked her awake with a finger. She stood, shuffled to bed, lay down with her hip touching Gail's. She plumped her fattest pillow and soon slept black sleep, no pictures were flashed in her head, no words were hollered, just black and sleep and the radiant heat raised by two lying close beneath the quilts.

ALL MORNING it seemed fiddlers hidden from sight played slow, deep songs and everybody in the house heard them and absorbed the mood of their music. The boys were broody, alert but broody and wordless as they ate the scrambled eggs and baloney Gail whirled together in the black skillet. Mom kept to her room and Sonny carried a plate to her. Ned gurgled in his carrier across the tabletop. The hidden fiddlers' music thickened the air with a lulling fog of low notes but now and then screeched rogue higher notes that raised eyes to the ceiling. Ree used her fork to chop her food to small bits, then gently chewed the bits on her unbroken side. Coffee made her broken side lunge with pain.

Sonny asked, "Will you see good again out of that swole eye?"

"They say."

"Is it still all the way blind now?"

She spoke mushmouth sentences through bloused lips. "I can tell the sun is up. Catch a shadow movin'."

Harold said, "There's two Miltons from over towards

Hawkfall in my grade — want I should fight the both of
'em?"

"No, Harold."

"I'm friends with one, but I'll still fight him anyhow if you
say."

"*No.* None of that. Don't do that. Not now."

Sonny said, "When, then?"

"If there comes a when, I'll tell you."

The boys split to catch their bus. Morning sun shined
everything wooden to gold and made a garish molten puddle
across the tabletop. Ree felt a dash of wooziness staring into
the puddle and pushed back from the table, rose, and sat in
Mom's comfy rocker. She swallowed the last white hysterectomy pills and hummed along with the fiddlers. The music
belonged to a ballad that the words to had been lost but was
still easy to hum. Gail stood in Ree's spot at the sink and
washed dishes slump-shouldered while staring out the window at the steepness of limestone and mud. Ree watched
Gail's strong back and scrubbing hands, then snapped to a
vision of herself idled by morning pills, beside the potbelly,
humming along with unseen fiddlers, and instantly began to
shake in Mom's rocker, shake and feel weak in her every part.
Weakened parts of her were crumbling away inside like mud
banks along a flood stream, collapsing inward and splashing
big flopping feelings she couldn't stand. She gripped fiercely
on the rocker arms and pushed and pushed until she gained
her feet, moved to a chair at the table, laid her head flat in the
molten puddle.

I ain't never goin' to be crazy!

Gail draped the dishrag over the faucet, turned around and said, "Done."

"You're awful good to pitch in."

Gail stood over Ned, adjusted his blankie, pulled his skull cap snug. "I've got someplace I want to take you, Sweet Pea. Someplace they say'll make you feel better in your bruises'n all."

"I don't know. I feel so stiff."

"Here. Take this." Gail reached into a near corner for a broom, an old grimy broom, the straw bristles trimmed short and made dull by long use. "You can lean on this ol' broom like a crutch, kind of. We'll be drivin', but there's *some* walkin'."

The broom helped. Ree put the straw end under her armpit and leaned. She tapped the broomstick to the floor and walked with a peg-leg sound to Mom's doorway. She rested against the jamb and squinted into the shadows.

"Mom, you might as well come out of your room. This is how I look now. I know it troubles you to see, but you might as well come out of your room'n get some sun. Your rocker's all warmed up for you. I'll only be lookin' this way for a while, then I'll be just almost like I was again."

Gail said, "You about ready?"

There was no response from the shadowed bed, no words or movement, and Ree turned away and thrust the broomstick down hard and creaked toward the front door. She took Mamaw's coat off the wall hook, slipped into the sleeves.

"Reckon I should bring my shotgun?"

"I would. If it happens you do need it, there ain't gonna be no time to send home for it."

"I about wouldn't mind needin' it today. I got me some targets picked out."

"Well, I hope to hell it don't come to that while Ned's along, that's all I can say."

"Aw, don't worry, they're probly done with me."

Ree carried the shotgun, Gail carried the baby. Ree limped on her broom down the porch steps to the old truck and noted a flurry of women watching from across the creek. Sonya, Betsy, and Permelia standing with two Tankersly wives from Haslam Springs and two women Ree didn't exactly recognize. Gail started the truck and eased down the rut road. She waved when level with the women across the creek.

Ree said, "What's up with them over there?"

"You, I bet. That's Jerrilyn Tankersly and, I think, Pam's her name."

"I know them two some — who's the other two?"

"One's a Boshell. I'm purty sure that's a Boshell. And one's a Pinckney girl who married a Milton. The tall gal's the Boshell. Both of 'em're from around Hawkfall."

"Think they're askin' shit about me?"

"Looks more like Sonya's *tellin'* 'em shit, from here. Their lips ain't movin' much."

Ree laughed, then winced when her hurt lips spread, and said, "Heck, none of the ones I'd like to shoot is standin' in the open over there. I could pot 'em from here if they was."

Gail twisted her neck to see the gathered women.

"Looks to me like Sonya's took up for you, Sweet Pea."

"Huh. She's got a soft spot for Sonny. Can't help herself."

At the hard road Gail continued south, straight across the

blacktop to regain the dirt rut. Barbed wire nailed to tilting timber posts made a slack fenceline along the western side of the rut. A roadkill armadillo had been tossed at the fence and snagged on a barb, tail up and eaten down to an eyeless husk that wiggled in the breeze. Gail said, "Does he know? Sonny?"

"Not from us. If he knows, it's from somebody else blabbin', 'cause we never." The eastern side of the rut belonged to the government and a wall of trees grew near the road. Branches overhead rent the sunlight into jigsaw pieces that fell to ground as a jumble of bright shards and deckled crescents. Beer cans and whiskey bottles and bread bags uglied the gully between the rut and the woods. Ree said, "The army'll still take you even without the full amount of teeth, won't they?"

"I don't know. I imagine they would. Why wouldn't they?"

Ned stretched and mewed, opened his eyes and puckered his lips, then was instantly asleep again. He smelled sweet and the trees stood tall and the truck jostled across furrows in the rut. Heavy clouds rimmed the northwestern distance, a warning border of bustling gray creeping into the plain sky.

"Blond Milton said him'n Sonya'd take Sonny. I tell you that? Raise him on up from here for me."

"He did? That might help some."

"But he'll make Sonny what I hoped he wouldn't be."

"Of course he will. That's why he wants him. That's why they all want sons. What about Harold?"

"Harold don't shine for him. Mom neither."

"Well, what else can you do? You thought about *that?*"

Pills shunted the pain aside from her body but did nothing for her pained thoughts but slow them to a yawning pace, make them linger. The shotgun was upright between her knees and she choked the double barrels with both hands. She said, "Carry Mom to the booby hatch'n leave her on the steps, I guess. Beg Victoria'n Teardrop to take Harold in."

Gail shook her head slowly, touched two fingers to Ned's chest.

"Oh, god, I hope that ain't the way it goes, Sweet Pea. I hope to hell it ain't. I don't believe Harold'll be the type can hack prison."

Ree stared ahead down the loose dirt rut while low dust dogs appeared alongside and chased the truck tires. The road was mostly straight and fairly smooth through the government trees. The truck crested a ridge and rolled downhill into a stark valley that narrowed to a springwater creek. Bluffs of dour stone shrugged above the bottoms, streaked black by ages of drip, with like boulders knocked low to the water's edge. The bluffs kept the creek shadowed but for two hours on either side of noon. Turkey buzzards spanned their wings and wafted in patient tightening circles high above the creek bed.

"Is *this* where you're takin' me?"

"Yup. Bucket Spring. Remember Bucket Spring? The water here's good for you."

"That water's colder'n hell!"

"That's what makes it good. That's what makes it help all your bruises'n bumps'n stuff."

"It's colder'n a goddam witch's tit in there!"

"Trust me."

Above the springhead there was a space to park, and logs pounded into the slope lengthwise made steps leading down to the clean, clean water. Where the spring boiled from the earth the water was a cool holy blue and rose to make jouncy plashes across the surface. As the water spread downstream the blue dimmed to crystal clarity and watercress grew in swaths of brilliant green along the bed. Boulders had fallen into haphazard stacks near the springhead and a few reached the pool of blue water and made angled sitting spots.

Gail helped Ree from the truck. Ree poked her way down the few dirt steps with their timber edges, leaning on the broomstick, while Gail carried Ned by the swinging handle of his carrier. They stopped on a gravel spit beside the pool.

"I'll make us a little fire, first. For when we come back out wet. You just rest 'til I get some heat raised, hear, Sweet Pea? Then we'll doctor you up good."

"Okey-doke."

"I'll set Ned here."

"Okey-doke."

The water was a color Ree'd pick for the jewel in a meaningful finger ring. She leaned on her broomstick, the end sinking into gravel, zoned still by pills and staring into the pool of jewel-colored water. Where the stream ran from the pool the water was so clear she could appreciate individual rocks on the bottom, clumps of green that swayed, skittish tiny fish facing upstream.

She sat on the spit next to Ned and stared. There was a metal ladle on a rope hanging from a sapling by the springhead, a ladle the old ones still came and dipped and raised to drink from the freshest of water. At school teachers said don't do that anymore, stuff has leaked to the heart of the earth and maybe soured even the deepest deep springs, but plenty of old ones crouched and sipped from the ladle yet. The pool of water loosed a scent, a blessed flavorful scent that folks couldn't often resist, something in the bones and meat made them bend, drink, step out and drop into the flow.

The fire was slow in starting, but Gail fed twigs to the first tiny flicker and calmly raised a fine strapping circle of flame. The smoke bent with the breeze and trailed away downstream, low above the creek. The fire flung heat as wide as two spread arms and Ned was set where the farthest hand would be. Gail said, "On your feet, Sweet Pea. Time to get naked."

"Other people could come here today, too, you know."

"Oh, goodness, I sure hope not — they'll see us both naked if they do."

Ree stood and dropped Mamaw's coat to the gravel spit, began to unbutton, and said, "I ain't swam naked since I don't know when."

"I bet the last time was in that pond over the ridge behind Mr. Seiberling's place. That was a purt-near perfect swimmin' hole, back before he started runnin' cattle and they filled it with flops."

"Yup. That was when."

Gail stripped to the buff quickly, then crouched to undo the laces of Ree's boots, tugged them off and set them near the fire. Ree stood bare to the wind, looking up at the tall dour bluffs. Her many bruises were changing colors by the hour, nearly, all of them hurtful to see. Gail took her hand and they stepped into Bucket Spring, waded straddle-deep into the chill water, and shivered and clattered, looking at each other with eyes popped wide until both began to laugh. Gail led on, pulling Ree toward the deeper blue center, feet shifting in the gravel underfoot, cold numbing legs to the hips. She dropped her haunches, water rose to her neck, and she said, "Sit."

"I already about can't feel my legs."

"Sit. Sit all at once'n get the shock over fast."

Ree let herself drop into the spring, sat cross-legged on the stone bottom. She lowered her face to the water and held her breath, letting the cold embrace her knotted features and sore spots. The cold went through her like wind. When she looked up she said, "Man! It blasts the hurt right out of you!"

"Don't it, though. Now get out'n get warm awhile. Then we do it again."

They stepped from the spring, hands rubbing at their skin. The pink on their bodies had become red and the white become pink and ringlets of splashed hair clung to their necks. They squatted near the fire, wore coats like cloaks draped around their shoulders, leaned toward the heat and watched the flames ripple.

Gail said, "I'm gonna go home."

"Home?"

"The trailer. Back to the trailer."

"You are? Back? Why?"

"Ned's gonna need more than me in this life, Ree. You had ought to know that real well yourself. Plus, you got all these troubles, and I sure shouldn't be in the middle of 'em, not with my baby along."

"I think most likely they're done with me."

"You can't know what's gonna happen. Me'n Ned need to get home."

Ree threw Mamaw's coat off, flung it at her piled clothes. She walked hunched over into the spring and fell in completely. She held her breath underwater and opened her eye and gained a clean misty view of rocks polished slick by ages and heard the murmur of a living spring in her ears, the mumbles and plops of water from forever rushing past. When she stood up, the breeze instantly made her soaked head too cold and she jumped from the spring toward the fire.

Gail said, "You're movin' better already."

"I forgot where I hurt."

"Might as well get dressed."

"Do you really love him or somethin'?"

"I don't know. My heart don't exactly bust out the trumpets every time I hear his name or nothin'. Nothin' like that — but I love Ned. I way, way love Ned."

Once dressed, Ree raised her broomstick but hardly needed to lean on it. She pegged to the truck, sat on the bench seat and swallowed a yellow pill and a blue pill. Gail drove in silence to the crest of the hill and over, out of the valley, back to the flat road through government trees. Buzzards had massed to peck something fluffy crushed on the road ahead but took off in gawky flapping alarm as the truck neared.

Ree said, "You didn't like it? You gonna tell me you didn't like it?"

"I liked it. I liked it, but not enough."

The glum front from the northwest had seeped gray over much of the sky. Huffing wind made the forest sway, and a brastle of limbs knocking was joined to the soughing. The road seemed three times as long going this way. A grunting timber truck passing slowly forced Gail to wait where the dirt met the blacktop. Red flags were tied to the log ends and foul smoke roiled from the tailpipe.

Ree said, "Think Floyd'n his daddy'd like to buy our timber from me? Huh? 'Cause if we got to sell, I'd rather it to be to you-all."

"Really? You mean that?"

They crossed the blacktop onto the rut road to home and Ree made herself look out the window the other way. "If I've got to sell these woods, Sweet Pea, I'd want it to be to you'n yours."

TWO KINDS of pills and a bedridden afternoon, evening, on into the night. The sky was dark and whistling, shaking windows and the horizon beyond, but Ree lay there immune to weather. The boys came home early and said, "More snow days!" but Ree merely grunted. The yellow pills had shown qualities worth appreciating, too. Seems like yellow ones shoved away hurt pretty good but left the mind on and lighted, while blue ones shut you down to an utter smooth blackness where time was sheared away in chunks without having to be lived through at all. Sometimes you want the mind on. Stuff dances around in there when the mind's on, not often the specific dancing memories you tried to call up with actual specific thoughts, but generally even the uninvited dancing stuff tickled or intrigued or at least left a fuzz of feelings behind. Whiteness piled on the windowsill, snowflakes sashayed and darted and plunged past the glass panes, and she reached to the floor bedside, shook loose another blue, and lay back waiting on black.

THE BLACK parted enough for a hand to reach through and shove her shoulder a few times, stand her up in her flannel nightie and knee socks and wrap Mamaw's coat around her. The dream did not tie her boots but turned into a truck ride, a truck ride through a white tunnel in the night, with white puffs dribbling across windshield glass and puddling below the wipers. She could smell Uncle Teardrop even through the veil of sleep. His smell and sounds were there, right there, but she was thinking in a gear so low she did not believe she could be awake until he touched her leg and his fingernail scraped a hurt place. She felt the pang through the pills, saw his face, the whiskey bottle held clenched by his thighs, the paratrooper's rifle and the sawed-off shotgun sliding on the cracked seat between his side and hers.

He said, "Let's do it then, girl. Fuck this waitin' shit. Let's get out'n poke 'em where they live a little bit'n see what happens."

Might be she said something, or maybe not, she wasn't sure, but he kept looking at her and his eyes were burnt spots in a flickering face. He nodded, so must be words had come from her mouth, though what she had agreed to eluded her, puzzled her, until a few possibilities came together as thoughts and scared her. She flinched and sat up a bit more. She rolled the window down and put her sluggish head into the cold wind. Places went past in a white hurry and were gone. She raised the window, faced him and asked, "What'd I just say?"

"Huh?"

"Did I just agree to somethin' or somethin'?"

"Haw-haw-haw, little girl. Don't try that smarty shit with me. We'll be there before long."

She realized with a start that she could again see from both eyes. The one eye afforded only a slitty sort of keyhole view but helped plenty to steady the scenery. There was not much to see except a wilderness of white, white fallen and white thrashing to ground. At road crossings she'd stare for clues as to where he was taking her. House lights and yard lights were vague daubs of glow. When the truck skidded onto a bridge and tires thumped on raised seams in the surface, she saw the water below. The water ate the flakes as they fell and was visible as a black neck between spread shoulders of white, and she knew that neck of water by sight, knew they'd crossed Big Chinkapin Creek.

She said, "Oh, no. Is this really the right idea?"

"Only one I got."

"You're goin' to Buster Leroy's house, ain't you?"

"I already told you that."

"I didn't hear you when you said it before."

"You heard me now." He raised the whiskey bottle and pushed it toward her, into her hands. "Have a snort'n buck up, girl. I been runnin' on crank'n hardly no food for fuckin' days now'n I'm tired of waitin' around for shit to happen."

She felt the burn in her throat and chest, then screwed the lid on and laid the bottle on the seat. He drove like the road was three lanes wide yet not quite wide enough. He drove the road from edge to edge and fast. The bottle rolled into her hip and she raised it for another swig at the top of a long hill, a long hill she thought they might well fly off of somewhere between here and the bottom. She closed her eyes and felt the swaying, sliding, heard the brakes heave, the gearshift grunt and Uncle Teardrop's laughter. She closed her eyes and went away on whiskey and pills, sunk into a shallow willed sleep that quickly deepened, and when her eyes opened again there was a farmhouse and a dog leaping at the window glass her face rested against, his teeth bared and his lips frothy inches from her own.

Teardrop stood on the steps of a wide porch to a stone house and the porch lights were bright. Snowflakes churned all around. The dog ran back to the porch snarling and he kicked it tumbling over shrubs into the snow, so it returned to leap at her face and growl. Somebody in a red T-shirt stood at the door, holding a handgun that he did not point at Uncle Teardrop but did gesture with, move up and down. She guessed Buster Leroy. She guessed . . . she heard the truck's tires crush fresh snow but wouldn't open her eyes, wouldn't when she heard a car horn honk, a mutt barking, gruesome laughter, wouldn't until motion ceased and voices sounded near and she saw two women and a man standing by the headlights, talking stuff with Teardrop. Snowflakes gushed across the headlight beams, blowing sideways now with smaller flakes that sounded like summer bugs mashing into the windshield.

The man laughed and made big gestures in the light. The two women pulled their jackets over their hairdos and huddled together. This was the parking lot of a gas station, the one at BB Highway and Heaney Cross Road that was also a market and pawnshop. Ree drifted, then knuckles rapped her window and she lowered the glass. The two women had come close for a look at her face, and she knew the closest of them, Kitty Thurtell, born a Langan, light in her bones and a mighty good mountain-style singer. Kitty said, "Oh, you poor whupped little kid, you — them Hawkfall gals sure 'nough beat the pee-waddy-do out your ass, didn't they?"

"Feels like it."

"Looks like it, too."

The other gal crouched to better see into the truck, and Ree recognized her as a Dolly, Jean Dolly from Bawbee. Jean lowered fogging stout eyeglasses and stared at Ree's marred cheek and fat lip, her head shaking as she crouched, then raised upright and said, "I once had my own ugly-fuckin' dustup with them lard-assed bitches. They ganged me the same shitty yellow-bellied way as they done her."

Kitty grabbed Jean by the arm, jerked, and said, "Don't you get too in the habit of sayin' that out loud that-a-way, hear me?"

"It needs sayin' out loud."

"Be careful where you say it, honey."

"I'll say the truth any-damn-where I want."

"Best say it in whispers about them."

The women turned from the wind and walked backwards

toward the gas station. Ree raised the window, leaned her face to the cold glass, and was quickly gone again. She was tucked into a blackness that was made incomplete by little pale lines of consciousness that buzzed around inside the black. When her eyes rolled open she was part of a cloud of some sort, a thick weary cloud that had settled to ground. Windows frosted and glazed, fog low outside the windows. Through the frost and fog there were red and green lights, and she scraped a peephole with a fingernail and saw a beer sign over the door to a cement-block building, an unpainted tavern with no windows or name but for the beer sign. Ree knew it as Ronnie Vaughn's place, and it probably had a proper name but she could not bring it to mind. Five or six vehicles were in the lot alongside the truck.

She was shivering, sniffling, and reached for the whiskey bottle. She drank and burped, then pushed the door open and stepped into the murmuring, fluttering weather. She pulled Mamaw's coat together over her flannel nightie and shuffled in untied boots to the tavern. As she stepped inside eight or ten bleary men looked her way. The kind of clodhopper music she couldn't stomach brayed from a garish jukebox and two mussed women standing far apart danced in wet boots. Teardrop glanced from the end of the bar, saw Ree, and pointed. He said to the bartender, "There she is now."

"She don't look all that terrible bad, man."

"If you saw the rest of her, she would."

Ree stood there, stoned sleepy and childlike, with Mamaw's coat fallen open to reveal her little flannel nightie and bruised shanks.

"That girl oughtn't be let in here, Teardrop. I mean, it ain't gonna be three full minutes before one of these drunk peck-erwoods takes a shine to her'n . . ."

The heated room of close withered air made Ree swoon. It was like all the air had been breathed many times before until shriveled and stinky from the mouths of chain-smoking drunks. She started to sit on a plastic chair but felt overcome by the place, the odors, the lights, that music, and she spun about instead and pushed outside again. The wind made her skin smart and she sat in the truck, leaned to the window, closed her eyes.

The truck started soon and Teardrop said, "Shit, girl, even lookin' beat up I could've married you off to three fellers in there. Interested?"

"I think I might puke."

"That's how I told 'em you'd be."

"Man — I'm gonna puke."

Teardrop drove onto the road invisible beneath stacking snow, goosed the truck to a jaunty pace. He glanced her way, said, "Upchuck out the fuckin' window, then. As much as you can, anyhow."

She thrust her head into the cold and broadcast the hot mush of old swallowed food toward the snowbanks. But wind turned the hot mush pouring from her mouth back onto the side of the truck and splats of puke melded to the fender. She hung her head out the window until her cheeks could not be felt and water drawn from her eyes thickened in her lashes. She pulled inside, raised the glass, let her head sag and eyes close. She said, "I ain't lookin' to marry."

Teardrop abruptly skidded the truck to a stop in the middle

of the fluffed white road. He stared into the rearview mirror while his thumbs tapped a short flourish of rhythm against the steering wheel. He drummed with his thumbs, looking in the mirror toward the beer sign lights behind him until he said, "I just don't think I like the way he said somethin'."

Teardrop clanged the truck into reverse and it whined as he pushed on the gas. He aimed for his own wheel ruts going backwards but twisted all over the road. He was going a bit fast for the turn into the tavern lot, so he just stopped where he was and got out, leaving the door flung open. He grabbed an ax from the truck bed, then walked through a border of drifts to the line of vehicles parked in the lot. They were all obscured by snow, and he walked along the line past two trucks and one car until he came to a certain large sedan. He cleared a hole and looked inside but seemed unsure. He then leaned across the hood and pulled the snow away with big sweeps of his arms, pulled until the front end was swept clear enough. He stood back, studied the grille and hood ornament, then raised the ax and crunched a hole through the front windshield. Snow sagged and sank inside the hole with the ruined glass. He hit the windshield again to speed the sinking, then casually returned to the truck, pitched the ax thudding into the bed. He got behind the wheel and said, "Sassy. Sort of sassy-soundin'."

Ree saw the tavern door open, and one, two, then three men stepped outside into the snow and watched as Teardrop drove away. She thought they might blast a few deer slugs or something toward Teardrop's truck, but these men made no gestures, yelled no words they wouldn't want heard. She faced backwards, watching them until they fell from sight. She turned forward, opened the bottle, had a quick drink.

"Can we go home? It's fuckin' cold out here, man."

"Those pills of mine Victoria gave you was what used to knock me off the mountaintop to sleep whenever I've been too far high too long like this."

"I didn't bring none."

"Can't catch no sleep by myself when I've clumb this high. Whiskey works, too, but slower."

"There's a few left at home, man."

The snowfall had nearly tuckered out but the wind remained brisk. They met three moving vehicles in ten minutes, and Ree spotted the yellow lights of a snowplow shoving along the main route distant in the valley. Teardrop left known roads and turned down little woodsy lanes Ree'd never seen before, spun tires up mounds and slid around curves. They made the first tracks everywhere. He finally turned at a flat white space between leaning rock columns, pulled past the columns a few feet and parked. It was an abandoned family cemetery on the back side of somebody's farm and headstones dressed with snow were lit by the high beams.

Teardrop said, "There's always been favorite places."

The headstones were the old sort that turned gray-green with time and often split in cold weather. They split at sharp angles, or fell apart in shards that were scattered by decades. More had fallen than stood. Ree stepped out of the truck to follow Teardrop's footsteps wending among the graves. Passing years had not rubbed the names to blank space on all the headstones and the name Dolly was in big letters on so many that Ree's skin spooked.

"Where the hell have we got to?"

Teardrop changed directions rapidly, stomping through the snow, first this way, then that, and she followed him, drunk in flopping boots. He stopped, held a hand to his ear, said, "This is where . . . I shouldn't say where this is."

"What're we doin'?"

"Lookin' for humps that ain't settled." He scanned the graveyard, his breath puffing hard from his mouth and flying toward the treetops. He crouched beside a headstone, held a flaring match to a cigarette, then blew smoke across the nearest name. He patted the stone, slid his fingers over the remaining letters, said, "It's a lonely ol' spot — that's what makes it a favorite place."

"You sayin' . . ."

"It's been done, girl."

She stumbled backwards, watching as his fingers tenderly traced the letters above the grave. She turned and felt a powerful need to run, run to the truck or farther, but her loose boots slipped from her feet and flew. She had to calm down in wet knee socks and hunt them in the snow. She carried the boots to the truck, got inside, and laced them tight, fashioned snug bows. She sat straight and stiff, raised the whiskey, poured.

When he sat in the truck, he said, "This ain't the right night. Snow."

"Uh-huh. All over."

He pulled from the graveyard, started back the way they'd come. Their path was rankled by ice clods and cracked branches. The snow had stopped and half the sky was the color of a spring pool and as clear. Ree looked to the stars shining so brightly, so plain and brilliant, and wondered what they meant, and if they meant the same thing as rocks in springwater.

"Can you push if we get stuck?"

"Not enough to help."

"You could drive, though, if I pushed."

"I've never had a car, man."

"I don't much feel like pushin', anyhow."

They reached the main route in the valley, drove closely behind a snowplow. The snowplow displayed bright yellow lights and the plow bellowed a dragon's roar scraping the road. A white fury was tossed up by the plow and made a hectic cloud of spindrift snow that broke low to ground and spewed. Teardrop turned the wipers on, then began to fall back from the snowplow. His eyes kept lolling shut, bursting open, lolling. When his eyes lolled, the truck hogged the center of the road. The snowplow was getting farther and farther ahead, and his eyes were about closed when flashing lights whirled over the truck from behind. Teardrop glanced in the rearview mirror but did not stop. A siren squawked briefly and he pulled over, rolled his window down, turned the wipers off.

Ree craned about to look out the back window. The flashing lights were dizzying and the headlights behind shined fiercely into the truck. She shielded her eyes and squinted. It was Baskin in a green deputy's coat and official smokey hat. He approached on Teardrop's side but halted at a distance of several feet and said, "Turn the engine off."

"I don't think so."

"Turn it off'n get out with your hands where I can see 'em."

Teardrop kept his head straight but angled his eyes to watch Baskin in the side mirror. His right hand eased toward the rifle. He said, "Nope. Tonight I ain't doin' a fuckin' thing you say."

Ree watched Teardrop's hand close around the rifle and she felt somehow instantly all sweaty on her insides, and her sweaty insides jumped into her throat. She saw Baskin drop a hand to his holster and step nearer the rear of the truck. Ree looked at the sawed-off shotgun on the seat between her uncle and herself and quaked.

In the brightness of lights and swirling colors, Baskin was mostly a shadow wearing a wide-brimmed hat. He said, "Get out, Teardrop. Get out now!"

Teardrop said, "Who'd you tell about Jessup, huh? You fuckin' prick. Who?"

For several seconds Baskin stood silently, his posture beginning to ebb, then inhaled hugely and drew his pistol from the holster.

Ree slid her fingers toward the shotgun, thinking, *This was how sudden things happened that haunted forever.*

"I've given you . . . that's a lawful goddam order. I've given you a lawful goddam order."

Sounds like singed laughter burst from Teardrop, and he jerked the rifle onto his lap, curled his trigger finger. He seemed to have caught Baskin's eye in the rearview mirror. He looked intently into the mirror, flicked a fingernail repeatedly against the folded wire stock on the rifle, *flick, flick, flick,* then said, "Is this goin' to be our time?"

Teardrop lifted his foot from the brake and calmly rolled

onto the scraped road and began to drive away toward home. Ree watched Baskin, and he stood alone there in the road behind with his pistol hand dangled to his side, then he crouched to a knee on the thinned snow in the gusting wind, facedown, and his hat popped off his head, but he caught it before it blew away.

THE BOYS had never known Mom when her parts were gathered and she'd stood complete with sparking dark eyes and a fast laugh. Mom only seldom walked farther than the kitchen and never danced during their days. Come morning, Ree saddled her hangover and rode that mood into the forlorn chores of a jittery day, and for over an hour she crouched at the big hall closet, pulling out dusty, tattered boxes of forgotten family flotsam, throwing everything away, until she came across a yellow envelope that held pictures. She spread the pictures on the floor and the boys bent over the snapshots, raising each for closer viewing, then dropping one old vision of Mom for the next. Mom in black-and-white, wearing a striped skirt that twirled aloft as she swung in the arms of Dad, sat on his lap beside a table overflowing with beer bottles and mashed smokes, did a tippy-toe spin on the kitchen floor with a full shot glass raised above her head. Mom in color, wearing a crown of twisted flowers at one of Uncle Jack's weddings, standing on the porch preened to go out for the night looking gorgeous in a red dress, a blue dress, a green dress, a slick black coat shiny as Sunday shoes. Her lips were ever painted bright and smiling.

Ree said, "She used to be so different from now."

Harold said, "Pretty. She was so pretty."

"She's still pretty."

"Not like then."

"And these fellas with her are all Dad."

Sonny said, "They are? That's him? Dad had hair like that?"

"Yup. It mostly fell out when he was away. You wouldn't remember."

"Nope. I don't remember him with much hair."

Her sad slumping task for the day was to begin sorting the house, go through closets and crawl spaces, haul forgotten boxes and bags into the light and decide what old stuff was to be kept and what would be burned in the yard as trash. Bromonts had been in the house for most of a century and some of the old boxes in out-of-the-way nooks had collapsed into fairly tidy heaps of so much rot. Many of the papers became powder in her fingers as she unfolded them for reading. There was a purple velvet jewelry box mice had chewed ragged, and she opened it to find a collection of marbles and a thimble and a Valentine's card received by Aunt Bernadette during third grade with words of love written large in crayon. She found heelless shoes still wrinkled from the feet of relatives who were dead before she could've known them. A large darkened knife with a bent blade. A delicate white bowl holding faded paper shotgun shells and a handful of keys to locks she couldn't imagine. Straw sun hats with brims torn away from the crowns.

"Carry this to the trash barrel'n start us a fire. Then come back — there's more."

Under the stairs she found several battered tools, ax blades, saw blades, awls and hammer shafts, cobwebbed jars of ancient four-sided nails with square heads, metal washers, bent drill bits. Schoolbooks with Mom's name printed in pencil inside the covers. A porcelain thunder mug cracked around the rim and base. A rusted lunch box lid that said *Howdy Doody!* and had the name Jack slapped on small with red fingernail polish.

Mom sat in her rocker, and Ree asked, "How much of what you got still fits?"

"These shoes do."

"I mean in your closet."

"Some in there never did."

Mom's closet was a jumbo mess of her own clothes, plus relics from Mamaw and Bernadette. Mom and Mamaw had both been of a mind to save anything and everything that might possibly be worn by somebody in the family someday or maybe have some other unknown future use. Mamaw had run to sloppy fat for her last many years, Bernadette was made short and scant, Mom long and lean. Not much that fit one ever would fit another, but the closet became stuffed with maybe-someday clothes and stayed that way. Most of the white things had long since yellowed on their hangers. Dust built yokes of grime on the shoulders of dresses and blouses.

Ree called the boys into Mom's room and both rushed to her side. They had a big jumping fire going in the yard and enjoyed feeding it all this Bromont trash. A circle of melt grew outward from the rusty barrel. Birds sat in black ranks on cozy branches above the gush of heated air. Ash crumbs wafted past the window and sprinkled gray dots across the snow. She said, "Hold your arms out'n I'll fill 'em with this junk."

She took a break and stood by the side window to watch the boys feed old family stuff to the fire. Across the creek, Sonya had come into her yard wearing a hooded overcoat and sat on the rock bench under her leafless walnut tree. It was very cold outside and the boys dodged about near the flames. Sonya waved and Harold saw her and waved back. Smoke boiled from the trash barrel, spilling a streaking mess into the valley. The boys held dresses above the barrel until they caught fire near the hem and the flames began to climb the cloth to the waist, the bodice, the neck, then dropped them at the last second before their fingertips blistered. Sonya waved and waved until Sonny finally saw her and waved back. Tiny bits of cloth rode the heat from the trash barrel up into the air, the edges briefly glowing as the last threads burned red, then became ash that matched the sky and disappeared downwind.

THEY CAME with the dark and knocked with three fists. The door shook as the clamor of beating knuckles filled the house. Ree glanced from a window and saw three like women, chesty and jowly, wearing long cloth coats of differing colors and barnyard galoshes. She fetched her pretty shotgun before opening the door. She jabbed the twin barrels toward the belly of Mrs. Thump, Merab, but did not speak. The shotgun felt like an unspent lightning bolt in her hands and trembled. None of the sisters flinched or stepped back or changed expression.

Merab said, "Come along, child — we're goin' to fix your problem for you." Her hands were in her coat pockets. Her hair was swept away from her face in a towering white wave that barely budged in the breeze. "Put that thing down. Show some smarts, child."

"Right now I feel like I want to blow me a *big sloppy hole* clean through your stinkin' guts."

"I know you do. You're a Dolly. But you won't. You'll put that scattergun down and come along with me'n my sisters."

"You think I'm crazy? I'd have to be crazy!"

"We'll carry you to your daddy's bones, child. We know the place."

The sisters were less stern versions of Merab. One had a shorter gray wave swept away from her face, standing stiff on top, and her cheeks powdered the pink of a faded rose. The other had a loosened wave of bottle-blond hair that shivered in the wind, and her fingers carried several knotty rings. They had faces like oaten loaves and flanked their sister with hunched shoulders, ready boots.

It was the blonde who said, "We ain't goin' to come back'n offer this again."

"You kicked me."

"Not in the face."

"Somebody did."

"Things got wild there for a bit."

Merab clapped her hands together, saying, "Come on! Come on along, now — it's cold. We need to put a stop to all this upset talk about us we've been havin' to hear."

"I ain't said a thing about you."

"We know. Everybody else has."

Ree moved the shotgun up and down. Her tongue licked over clotted vacancies between teeth. She heard the boys come to the door and stand behind her. "Get back in the house. Keep out of sight." She poked the shotgun forward, said, "I'm bringin' this."

"No, you won't either bring that. You want his bones, you'll set that down'n come along."

There was that scrape of unbidden music in her head, the beginning of a tilt, but she hushed the fiddle with a sharp

thought and spread her boots for balance. She stood the shotgun in the corner behind the door, grabbed Mamaw's coat
from the hook and led the way down the porch steps. The sisters walked behind her like guards. The car was a four-door
sedan with dulled paint and plenty of heft and iced snow on the
roof. The quietest sister reached into her pocket for a burlap
tote sack she shook open, then handed to Ree. "You can't
know where we're takin' you to. You'll have to wear this over
your head. It's clean. Don't try'n look out from under, neither."

"You fixin' to shoot me?"

"If you think a minute, you'll know we could've did that
already if we wanted."

Merab said, "Sit in back with Tilly."

Tilly was the blonde. Ree slid onto the seat and pulled the
tote sack down. Tilly reached over to adjust the burlap, make
sure no scrap of sight remained. The sack smelled of old oats
and sunshine and scratched against her skin as the car hit
bumps. The car had a big engine and leapt across some potholes and punished others with its pounding weight. The
sack worked loose and she could breathe better, see a crack of
light. She inhaled the scent of the sisters, a domineering reek
of udder balm and brown gravy, straw and wet feathers. The
car fishtailed in spots and skidded when turning.

Merab said, "Dammit — don't slam the brakes — tap
'em."

"I don't want to tap 'em. I don't tap."

"You ain't s'posed to slam 'em on snow."

"When it's your car, you can tap 'em. I drive *my* car just
exactly this way."

"These roads're slicker'n you seem to think."

"Look, when I wreck, you can tell me all about why. 'Til then, change the subject."

Ree tried to guess where they were. It all depended on that first turn from the hard road — was that by the school? Or was it closer than that? One way meant Bawbee, the other should mean Gullett Lake. Unless the turn was *past* the school. The turns began to come too quickly to divine, and Ree became altogether lost among the crossroad possibilities and confusing maybes.

Tilly said, "Speed up, huh? I'd like to be home for my program."

Inside the hood, Ree came to know the flavors of her own wind. The sound of her own bellows at work. The whistling breaths and smells that were her. She was loudly alive in her own ears and okay to smell.

"That funny one?"

"I never find it all that funny."

"Then which one do you mean?"

"The one you call the funny one. I just don't find it to be all that funny. What I like is the puppet that lives in the basement."

"You remember to bring gas for the chain saw?"

"It's got gas. I looked at home."

The bounces became higher. Tires grunted across some uneven surface, a field, a cow path, the rippled earth of a river bottom. During the higher bounces Ree and Tilly bumped together.

The car eased to a stop, and Merab said, "Get the gate."

"Should I latch it back? Or wait 'til we leave?"

"We'll latch it leavin'."

Beyond the gate, the car was driven more slowly, meaning there must not be much of a road beneath the tires. There came a stretch of jolting, rhythmic jolting, the jolts all alike, and Ree guessed they were driving sideways over a cornfield. There was an extra noise that could be the dry crack of corn stalks breaking.

"Where's the path?"

"Over under them trees."

"Park there."

Tilly maneuvered Ree out of the car, holding on to an arm and pushing. The air was cold and had a little slap to it and the sack ruffled. The snow was crusty underfoot, an iced layer of crunch thin on top. Somewhere distant a train neared a crossroad and hooted a warning. The trunk popped open; things were lifted out. Ree stood straight and proud in case the very worst was about to happen and she would soon be presented to the Fist of Gods, and no god craves weaklings.

Merab said, "When I take this sack off your head, you might know where you are. I don't really think you could, but if you *do* know where you are, you forget you know it. Get me? Don't try'n guess where this is, or ever come back here if you know. That won't be allowed." The sack was removed with a yank and tossed onto the backseat. Tilly shouldered an ax, the other sister hefted a small chain saw. Merab held a heavy flashlight that threw a long beam. "There's still a little walkin' to get there. Follow me."

A field, a line of trees, a small path with a few paw prints wending deeper into the woods. A plump waxing moon and silvered landscape. Merab followed the beam and led them on a slow wamble across a rankled field, then a slight curving path rose to a balled mound with a knuckled ridge and down again into a vale. It was a coggly path to an iced pond, with a hedge of blowdown barring the way. The logs and branches caused slipping and barked shins, oaths and mutters, but were soon put behind, and the women gathered into a puffing rank, staring down at the stiffened pond.

Merab said, "There he is, child. See that tallest little willow? Your dad's sunk under it, tied to an engine block."

The pond in silver light, with the slouched willows and surface of dull ice, instantly became a wrenching vista. Cattails and small nibbling fish in low water, a living grave for Dad. An urge to kneel on the snow waterside passed in a sniff, and Ree moved around the bank toward the tallest little willow. She slipped on the snow, stood, stepped, slipped again. The sisters followed her around the pond to the spot nearest the willow.

Merab said, "I'll shine the light. You'll need that ax to open the ice."

"Then what?"

"He ain't deep. This water don't get deep."

Ree stomped the ice and it creaked but did not crack wide. She took another step, and another, then came back for the ax. She stood on the ice near the willow, raised the ax and put all her feelings into the whacks she delivered unto that pond. It sounded like grievous hammering, hammering met with slushy grunts as the ice shattered and black water splashed.

The light shined where the ice had been and freed water heaved.

"He's right there, child. Underfoot, almost."

"I don't see him."

"You've got to reach down'n tug him up for seein'. He ain't floatin' no more, but he won't seem heavy."

Ree removed Mamaw's coat and flung it toward Tilly. She dropped to her knees and edged over the ice to the open place. She plunged her arm into the pond and screamed, screamed at the cold, but moved her hand all around. Her hand quickly felt thickened, insensitive and balky, so she pulled it out and stuck in the other.

"Go straight down, not over to the side like that."

She felt something, something cloth, pulled hard. The light was partial but the main spot was bright. She knew that shirt. A green plaid flannel with the sleeves hacked off at the shoulders. Long johns underneath, with long white sleeves. The long johns felt like mud or moss or both in her hand. She tugged until she saw an ear, then turned her head and puked at the willow. She did not let go as she spewed.

"Here's the chain saw."

"What?"

"How else you goin' to get his hands? They'll know it's him by his hands."

"Oh, no, shit. No."

"Take the saw — here."

"No, no."

The quiet sister held the light. Merab sighed big and loud, then came onto the ice lugging the chain saw and crouched beside Ree. "Don't think of him as your daddy — just some guy. He's just some guy."

Tilly said, "Look away from his face."

Merab said, "Jesus, shit, we'll be here all night the way you're doin'." She jerked the saw started and leaned toward the shirt. "Hold his arm out straight, child, and I'll make the cut."

The saw pissed smoke and rattled and the smoke made dread wisps over the ice and the rattles filled the night. Flecks of meat and wet bone hit Ree in the face and she closed her eyes and felt patters on her eyelids. When the blade cut through, Dad's body sank away from her grasp but she had his hand from the wrist. She spun and tossed it onto the bank near the sisters.

Merab said, "Why'd you let go? You'll need *both* hands or sure as shit they'll say he cut one off to keep from goin' to prison. They *know* that trick. Reach back down there, now — quick. And be careful of his skin — that's your fingerprints. Your proof."

The ice gave as she stretched, and she fell into the pond. She felt Dad with her legs, bent into the water and raised him by pulling on his head. His skin felt like pickled eggs. She found the good hand and pulled it toward the chain saw. Her body was gone, she could not feel it below the neck, and a glow spread in her mind. She was on a distant tranquil shore where rainbow-colored birds sang and coconuts dropped bountifully to warm sand. The smoke and rattle, his other hand coming free, the return walk to the car a blur. The sisters peeled her soggy clothes from her frame and shoved her into Mamaw's coat.

Dad's hands brought sorrow and a blessing. Deputy Baskin was called and came for the hands the next morning. The sky was piled with bland clouds. Ree and Baskin met on the porch and he stared at Ree, wearing his big hat, with his lips rumpled, pinched tight. Dad's hands bulged the blindfold-sack, and the burlap was still damp. Baskin said, "How in hell'd you come by these?"

"Somebody flung 'em on the porch last night."

"They did? They knock first?"

"Nope. I heard the thump. Got up. Found 'em."

"Uh-huh. I'll go on'n act like I believe that, girl, out of regards for your grief'n stuff. You know, truth is, a lot of the time I actually sort of liked ol' Jessup. He wasn't always all that bad to be around. He could tell a joke good, at least. Amen." He opened the sack, looked inside, twisted it closed again. "I reckon I'll run these paws straight in to town, have the doc tell me if they're his."

"They're his, man. It's Dad's hands."

"We'll know yes or no on that soon enough." Baskin stood with his legs spread and his teeth nibbling at his dry lips, the burlap sack swaying. The brim of his hat shaded his eyes. "I didn't shoot the other night 'cause you were there, you know. In the truck. He never backed me down."

"It looked to me like he did."

"Don't you start sayin' that to folks around here, girl. Don't let me hear that's the story gettin' around."

"I don't talk much about you, man. Ever."

He rolled the sack tight, rolled it into a compact brown bundle, and stomped down the porch steps. Without looking back at her, he said, *"Sometimes I get so fuckin' sick of you god-dam people, know it?"*

When the boys came home from school she told them that Dad was gone for good, dead, they wouldn't see him again, not in this life. Both boys said they already pretty much knew, and Harold asked what heaven was like. "Sandy. Lots of fun birds. Always sunny but never way hot."

The next day she cleaned Dad's shed. Rakes and hoes stood in a corner. A punching bag of battered red leather hung chained from a wooden beam. The swaying chain had dug a deep groove into the wood. She kicked the bag. The chain rattled and she remembered how happy she always used to get hearing Dad whip that bag, rattle that chain, make the bag jump. The first year after he came home from the pen he'd spent hours and hours out here, day after day, punching away. He called the bag Hagler and taught her to punch it, too. The leather scraped her bare knuckles raw, and the gloves were so heavy she'd had to wind up ridiculously to heave even a slow round punch. The gloves still dangled by their laces from a nail in the wall.

When the boys came home she met them in the doorway, holding the gloves.

"Another thing you two'll want to know, is how to fight. I can show you what Dad showed me. Knock the spiderwebs out of them gloves and I'll lace you both up."

The boys were very concerned about spiders, spiders inside the old gloves that'd come awake smelling the sweet blood in their young fingers and scurry from cracks in the stuffing to bite. They swatted the gloves against the wall, the potbelly, held them upside down and shook, stuck table forks inside and poked around. Ree pulled the gloves onto their hands, wrapped the laces around their wrists and tied them. Their hands were too small for the gloves but she tied the laces tight so they'd hold. She showed them the basic stance, left foot forward, left fist forward, right fist held back cocked beside the ear.

"Let your weight come along behind your punches, that's" — she looked from the window to see Uncle Teardrop drive into the yard — "hang on a minute." She held the door open for her uncle. The boys did not wait for further instructions, but leapt together and began belting each other, swinging and sliding on the wooden floor, ducking behind the couch, the chairs, shrieking as they hit and got hit. Teardrop came into the loud house looking tired, hair limp and uncombed, days of whiskers making his cheeks seem blued, wearing black pants with mud daubs at the cuffs. She tapped his arm, said, "Hey — have a seat."

He watched the boys with interest. They flailed away with the heavy gloves, and both reddened in struck spots but neither bled. They began to tire quickly, swinging wild blows that fell three feet short of each other, and puffing.

"Bell," she said. "You sit between rounds."

Teardrop said, "How is it now over here?"

"Mom's not good." Ree gestured toward Mom's shadowed room. "I think she knows."

"I expect she knows more'n any of us think."

"More'n she wants, anyhow."

The boys were beside the kitchen sink, trying to get glasses from the cupboard while still wearing boxing gloves. Their cheeks were flushed and Harold sniffed. They punched the faucet open and held the glasses with bunched mitts.

"I guess you'll be needin' to get some money laid by. I could scare somethin' up for you, girl, learn you how to earn around here."

"I won't touch crank. Crank ain't for me. Nobody gets better from that shit."

"There's other stuff to do, too, if you'll do it."

"You boys sit still a minute. I'll turn the TV on. Sit."

The picture was fluttery, lines dashing about and warping, but the program was explained by a news announcer's words, and Teardrop sat on the couch to watch. The boys sat at one end, slurping water, Teardrop at the other, and they sort of saw but mostly heard about big events off in other corners of the Ozarks.

The main news, the news of the world, was just beginning when headlights approached on the rut. Mike Satterfield parked beside the truck and came across the snow, swiping at his long brown hair. He carried a blue plastic sack and had a pistol strapped to his leg. She let him inside without any greeting but a nod. He saw Teardrop on the couch, said, "I know you, don't I?"

"Yup. Mike, ain't it? Crick's boy. I've known ol' Crick since my whiskers came in fuzzy."

"Is that when you posted your first bond?"

"Before that, even. He used to do my daddy sometimes."

Satterfield studied Ree more closely in the weak light, said, "Looks like you earned this with blood, kid." He handed the blue sack to her. "This is yours."

The sack was fat with crinkled bills.

"How's it mine?" He sat sideways to the window and sundown, and his eyes threw tiny sparks of color. His chin hair was one step lighter than his head hair and his knuckles were stout and he smelled like town. "Ain't it his?"

"The fella with no name? He never gave a name and, hell, I couldn't say for sure the man was ever even all the way awake, but he was sure 'nough good news for you-all when he put this down on Jessup."

Teardrop stood straight up and walked outside.

Ree said, "Ain't it still his, though?"

"Ol' no-name ain't hardly gonna come back for it, not the way things happened. We took our cut from the cash, and there's this much left. That makes it yours."

The boys sensed something special had occurred and stood at Ree's side with their boxing gloves on her shoulder. They peeked into the bag, and Harold said, "Does this mean you're leavin'?"

Teardrop's pacing steps thudded on the porch planks.

Satterfield said, "I don't know how you did it, kid. How you got out there'n run down the *proof* and all. Not many could do that. You're somethin', kid."

Words weren't forming for her, they skittered away, but finally she snatched a few and said them. "Bred'n buttered. I told you that."

"Does this money mean you're leavin'?"

Satterfield leaned to her, swatted his hair, shook her hand. "Listen, kid, you ain't old enough to hire legal'n all that, I know, but if you could get around, drive to town'n places, we'd sure use you. We go the bail for most every Dolly this side of the Eleven Point, you know. Almost all of you-all get bonded out by us. You'd be like gold to me."

Shadows were long across the yard as Satterfield left. Birds gathered all about in the trees and made their shrill evening noise. She stood on the porch, watching him drive away, then turned to Teardrop. The color of him had changed, paled, paled everywhere but his scar. His hands were jammed deep inside the pockets of his slashed leather jacket. She said, "What? What's the matter?"

"I know who now."

"Huh?"

"Jessup. I know who."

Without hesitation or thought she sprang to him, spread her arms and held him tightly, smelled the raw scent of him, the sweat and smoke, the roiling blood and spirit of her own. She felt she was holding somebody doomed who was already vanishing even as she squeezed her arms around his neck. The shadows had the creek, the valley, the yard, the house. The shadows were over them and she wept, wept against her uncle's chest. She wept, snuffled, wept, and he hugged her, hugged her 'til her backbone creaked, then broke away. He went down the steps three at a time, hustled to his truck without a backward glance, and was gone.

She sat on the top step trying to dry her eyes with a sleeve. The birds had so much to say at dusk and said it all together. She laid two fingers high on her nose and pinched a yellow splat to the yard. Ice hung in glaring jags from the roof, poised like a line of spears above the steps. Snow on the steps had been beaten flat by winter boots and become hardened and slick. The boys sat on both sides of her, leaned their heads to her chest, rested boxing gloves in her lap.

Harold said, "Does this mean you're leavin'? That money?"

"I ain't leavin' you boys. Why do you think that?"

"We heard you once, talkin' 'bout the army and places we wouldn't be. Are you wantin' to leave us?"

"Naw. I'd get lost without the weight of you two on my back."

They sat quietly, the shadows deepening, lights shining in windows across the creek.

Sonny said, "What'll we do with all that money? Huh? What's the first thing we'll get?"

Fading light buttered the ridges until shadows licked them clean and they were lost to fresh nightfall. The birds quieted as the last light darted away. Ree stood and stretched. Twilight dimmed the snow, but icicles overhead held that gleam.

"Wheels."

ABOUT THE AUTHOR

DANIEL WOODRELL was born in the Missouri Ozarks, left school and enlisted in the marines the week he turned seventeen, received his bachelor's degree at age twenty-seven, graduated from the Iowa Writers' Workshop, and spent a year on a Michener Fellowship. *Winter's Bone* is his eighth novel. His five most recent novels were selected as *New York Times* Notable Books of the Year, and *Tomato Red* won the PEN West Award for fiction in 1999. He lives in the Ozarks near the Arkansas line with his wife, Katie Estill.

Acknowledgments

Thanks are due to my editor, Beverly Reingold, and my agent, Alison Picard; to oboist Catalina Arrubla; to my longtime friend, Brooklyn native Gregory William Frux, who introduced me to the evocative neighborhood surrounding the Gowanus Canal and supplied many details about the setting; and to my friends and family who read and critiqued early drafts: Jeannine Atkins, Bruce Carson, Lisa Kleinholz, Nancy Kaplan, Philip Kaplan, Shel Horowitz, Susan Friedman, Stanley Friedman, Alana Horowitz Friedman, and Rafael Horowitz Friedman.